NO DIVING
AND OTHER STORIES

NADIA HOOPER

For my Family

To Ruth,
My little book!
With love,
Nadia x

CONTENTS

AN HONEST WOMAN

The endless display counters in the large department store glistened with an array of earrings, bracelets and cufflinks. She wandered around, coyly, past eagle-eyed sales assistants who paced like predators waiting on their prey.

Presently, she found herself drawn to a friendly-looking man with a carrot complexion and welcoming smile. He stood beside a gilt-framed sign on the counter that boasted 'The Perfect Gift for the One You Love.'

'May I help you madam?' he said, his smile broadening to reveal perfect white teeth.

'I do hope so. I'm looking for a gift for my husband. It's his birthday next week and I thought perhaps a pair of cufflinks...'

'Well, madam, you've come to the right place,' he said, cutting in with animated enthusiasm. 'As you can see, we have a wonderful selection. It does of course depend on your husband's taste. For instance, does he favour something colourful, or more subtle, like these?' He ran a finger lightly back and forth along the counter to illustrate the various styles, then discreetly inspected it for dust. 'Would madam like to take a closer look?'

'Yes, thank you.'

He opened the cabinet and carefully removed a tray lined with quilted black satin, on which several rows of cufflinks were laid out. He placed it on top of the counter and with a theatrical sweep of his hand, presented them to her. He remarked on their uniqueness and the way the light bounced off the different patterns and textures, but her eyes settled on just one pair.

'These, I like these,' she said pointing, almost touching them, her delicate hand faintly trembling.

'Sapphire. An excellent choice madam, if I may say so.' His eyes widened with excitement, his smile steadfast.

'How much are they?' she asked with the nonchalance of the well heeled.

'These, madam...' - he squinted as he read the small price tag that dangled from one of them – 'These are one thousand pounds, but today we are offering a ten per cent discount to all our customers.'

'Oh!' she exclaimed, her voice shrill, quenching any hint of affluence, 'It's rather more than I wanted to spend. What a shame.'

'Well, they *are* gold and sapphire.' He spoke the words proudly, as though they had been crafted by his own hand. 'Madam, please examine the detail, the work that has gone into them, how truly exceptional they are.'

He held them under her nose, as one would a scented flower.

'When he sets eyes on these he will love you forever!' he said jubilantly, implying that the deal had been struck.

'Oh yes, they are beautiful, but I'm afraid they're still out of my price range.'

'Madam has a budget,' he said, clearly deflated now. 'Then I expect madam would like to see something else. Something more suited to her pocket,' he said, almost spitting the words. 'How much *does* madam wish to spend?' He proffered a benevolent smile, though it failed to mask his disenchantment.

'Well, no more than a hundred pounds really,' she replied apologetically.

His nostrils flared as if he had detected a foul odour, the smile swiftly replaced by a sneer.

'Well, we have a limited selection. Here.' He tapped his finger dismissively on the glass at a tray of inferior-looking cufflinks, before scooting around the counter to appease a well-dressed woman who was furiously flapping for attention, in his haste omitting to replace the tray. She bit on her lower lip and stared longingly at the sparkling sapphire.

Outside on the street she leant against the wall to catch her breath, all the time looking furtively to and fro, before continuing on her way. She marched as fast as her feet would carry her, until at last she reached the entrance to her apartment building. She ran along the hall and fled up the stairs, frantic as she fumbled in her handbag for her keys, her heart beating wildly. Once inside, she closed the door and dropped to her knees, brimming with a mix of fear and elation as she took the cufflinks from her coat pocket. She was not a criminal. She was an honest woman. She kept telling it to herself,

3

hoping it would somehow atone for her crime. She pictured her husband's face and the look of delight when he opened the box, then hid the cufflinks in a drawer where she was sure he would not find them.

'Happy Birthday dear,' she said, handing her husband the small box that she had exquisitely wrapped in gold paper.

'For me? You shouldn't have!' he said, his face flush with anticipation.

She smiled lovingly, but as she watched him unwrap the box, every beat of her heavy heart served as a reminder of her transgression.

'Cufflinks!' he exclaimed. 'Wonderful.'

'Do you like them? They're sapphire and gold.'

'Of course I like them darling. I love them, but...' he hesitated while he examined them more closely, 'I can't keep them. They must have cost a fortune. It was a lovely gesture, but we'll have to return them. There's nothing else for it.' He smiled ruefully, his expression sombre now, no sign of the joy of only moments before.

'Oh, but you've got to keep them, you've simply got to!' she said, a feeling of abject terror growing in her. 'Promise...promise me you'll keep them. It's your birthday and I want you to be happy. Please, let's be happy. It would break my heart to return them.'

As the days passed she tried not to think about what she had done, but the guilt consumed her and soon the guilt turned to fear, fear that she would encounter the sneering assistant on the street or somewhere, anywhere. She thought of how she was always bumping into people she knew, especially when she hadn't wanted to and how just as easily she might bump into him. If only she could turn back the clock and undo the whole sorry business. But she couldn't. She would have to tell her husband and even though she was sure his response would not be one of anger, it would instead be one of unimaginable disappointment, which was far worse. He was a good man, a kind man, a man of the utmost integrity and she had failed him. She had no choice but to confess.

At first he didn't believe her, could not imagine his wife was capable of such a thing, but her tears, accompanied by a look of utter despair, were proof enough of her crime and his expression conveyed all she needed to know.

The next day she returned to the shop with the cufflinks. They looked untouched, wedged into the velvet pad that sat snugly inside the wine-coloured box, and she felt somehow less culpable, in the knowledge that her husband had not worn them.

She approached the assistant, full of dread and prepared for her fate. He looked up and smiled the same inviting smile, a glint in his perfect white teeth.

'I'll be with you in just a moment madam,' he said, turning his back to deal with another customer. He didn't seem to recognise her. She felt sure that he would remember her, would have some recollection of her, or the fact of her relatively modest means and she wondered how long it would be before the smile was replaced with a sneer, just as it had been on that fateful day.

'Sorry to have kept you madam. How can I help?'

Suddenly she realised that he had absolutely no idea who she was, let alone that she had stolen the cufflinks and she wondered then if he had even noticed they were missing. Her head was spinning as she decided what to do next.

'Madam is not sure. What exactly did madam have in mind?'

She stood, frozen to the spot, searching his eyes for a hint of recognition, but he just looked at her and smiled.

'Perhaps madam needs more time,' he said.

'No. I…'

All of a sudden she blurted it out, a panic-stricken effusion of words, as though led by a force beyond herself. She told him how she had come to the shop in search of a gift, how she had been looking at the tray of cufflinks. He shook his head and she could tell by the look of bewilderment on his face that he still had no recollection of her. She went on to say how she must have inadvertently swept the cufflinks into her bag with the wide sleeve of her navy blue overcoat, because she found them a week later, concealed in the ripped lining of a large side pocket. She calmly handed him the box, but as she did so, she knew, from the beads of perspiration streaming steadily down the side of his face, to the look of absolute terror in his eyes, that he had not even realised the cufflinks were missing.

'Good heavens!' he blurted out, his eyes widening with disbelief. 'Madam, what an honest woman you are. I am becoming so forgetful of late. I should have noticed they were gone. I should have known. How could I not have known?' He looked at her with a touching desperation, tears welling up in his eyes as he beseeched her for an answer. 'I've had so much on my mind these past weeks. Mother has been quite ill and it hasn't been easy. And sales...sales have been poor. Madam, I implore you, I would be most grateful if we kept this to ourselves. You do understand, don't you?'

She felt driven by a harrowing sense of guilt, coupled with pity, to tell him that she had stolen the cufflinks, but she knew she mustn't. Chance had delivered her from a most unfavourable outcome.

She prayed that her husband would find it in his heart to forgive her. After all, he was a good man, a kind man, a man of the utmost integrity and she was an honest woman.

THE DINNER PARTY

The Wades were coming to dinner, much to Penelope's displeasure. She cared little for their company and even less for the inevitable small talk. But above all, she resented having to watch her husband Nicholas flap and fawn over Mrs Wade like a lovelorn teenager.

They had become acquainted with the Wades some years earlier while on holiday in Cyprus, when Nicholas had pursued them with the kind of tenacity that could only be described as akin to a stalker. He gushed over Mrs Wade all week and in an effort to keep her in his radar, feigned friendship with her husband.

Amanda Wade was the stereotypical object of male desire – beautiful, curvaceous, flirtatious and more importantly, unavailable. But there was another string to her seductive bow; the well honed giggle, coquettish and delivered in a manner that sent Nicholas into spasms of boyish delight.

When the doorbell rang, Nicholas was studying his reflection in the hall mirror, spitting on his hand and carefully flattening a few strands of stray hair over his receding pate. He opened the door and there was Amanda, wrinkling her nose and smiling girlishly. Beside her, attempting to mask his dour expression, stood her husband Charles. Nicholas reached for his hand and shook it cordially, but all the while his eyes were fixed on Amanda.

Penelope was standing at the end of the hall in her apron, looking flustered. She waved at them with an egg whisk, as though she was conducting an orchestra, just making out Amanda's tightly clad silhouette in the dimness of the hall light.

When she joined them in the drawing room, Nicholas was pouring champagne into Amanda's glass, at the same time stroking the soft white flesh of her upper arm and telling her how lovely she looked.

'He never says that to me anymore,' Penelope said acerbically.

'Really?' Amanda replied with a quizzical look, her lips puckered in an expression of pity.

'Yes, really.'

As the evening dragged on, Nicholas's enthusiasm reached fever pitch, his eyes gleaming with each compliment that came his way, especially when Amanda told him how much she loved his shirt, the very shirt that Penelope loathed. The praise flew back and forth, Amanda blushing with delight when he admired her choker and the way it sat so beautifully on her swan-like neck, complementing her ivory skin, while Penelope shook her head in exasperation and Charles uttered not a single word.

By the time they finished dinner, they had polished off several bottles of wine and Amanda, having tired of teasing Nicholas with her customary come-hither routine, segued into more perilous territory.

'I've got a wonderful idea!' she exclaimed, her eyes widening with mischief, 'Why don't we all go back to Cyprus? It would be such fun.'

'What a splendid idea,' Nicholas replied, flush with excitement.

'I have an even better one,' Penelope said, looking daggers at Amanda. 'Why don't you and Nicholas go back to Cyprus and Charles and I can go elsewhere. That way we wouldn't spoil your fun, would we Charles?'

'Penelope!' Amanda squeaked in a shrill voice.

'Darling!' Nicholas gasped, as if the mere thought of it horrified him.

'But wouldn't that just suit you, darling? What do you think Charles? You're keeping tight-lipped. Surely you have something to say on the matter.'

Charles let out a quiet sigh and looked away. Penelope turned to Amanda.

'And you Amanda, what do you say?'

'I say we all go together,' Amanda said girlishly.

Penelope threw her hands up as she stood to clear the plates.

'Can I do anything to help?' Amanda said with a peculiar urgency.

'I don't think so, but if you feel you must.'

She followed Penelope into the kitchen, Penelope silently berating herself for her unusual rancour. Few people had the ability to nettle her, but Amanda was one of them.

It had all began with their first meeting at the poolside restaurant of the Hotel Constantina. Amanda was posing provocatively in a lime green bikini, with a flesh coloured sarong tied loosely at her hips. Nicholas looked at her as though he had never seen a woman before, his eyes scrutinising her full breasts, which were encased in two small triangles of fabric precariously restrained by a halter strap no thicker than a shoe lace. She introduced herself, while her husband, his face buried in a newspaper, so that only a dense mop of light brown hair was visible, nodded his acknowledgement.

That evening, not wishing to bump into them again and much to Nicholas's vexation, Penelope suggested dinner at a bistro in the local town. But when they arrived, Amanda and Charles were sitting at the bar, sipping cocktails.

It wouldn't have been as bad if Charles had not been quite so taciturn. At least they could have railed together against their errant spouses. But it was not to be and so, instead, Penelope spent the rest of the week propped up at the pool bar, phrasebook in hand, teaching the barman a few choice words in English with which to charm the women, in exchange for several new concoctions.

Up until then, Nicholas had seldom expressed interest in maintaining holiday friendships and in spite of Penelope's disapproval, insisted they keep in touch with Amanda and Charles, almost imploring them to come for dinner one evening. And so, his burgeoning infatuation was to continue.

'You do know how my poor husband feels about you? I mean, you'd have to be blind not to,' Penelope said calmly as she loaded the plates into the dishwasher.

Amanda looked at her dolefully.

'I don't think we've ever had a proper conversation, have we Amanda?' she continued. 'Then again, we really have nothing in common, apart from my husband of course?'

'I had hoped we'd have got to know one another better by now,' Amanda said.

'Oh?'

'I know I'm not your favourite person but...'

'Do you?' Penelope replied, a look of bemusement on her face.

'The thing is, you don't really know me at all, because if you did, you might feel less inclined to judge me and, who knows, in time you may even learn to like me,' Amanda said, not a hint of the girlishness that so enamoured Nicholas.

'Well, you give me little reason to,' Penelope replied.

'Then perhaps what I am about to tell you will change your mind, because only then might you understand the frivolousness of my flirtations with your husband,' Amanda said solemnly.

'I rather doubt it, but fire away.'

'You see my darling husband is having an affair.' She spoke the words with an eerie composure.

Penelope turned to look at her, open-mouthed with disbelief.

'Good God! Are you sure? Quiet little mousy Charles?'

'Oh I'm sure. It's been going on for years.'

'Then why on earth didn't you say anything before?'

'Because I hoped he'd have ended it by now, but he hasn't. I've thought about leaving him more times than I can say, but there wouldn't be much point, since I can't imagine my life without him.'

'Well, I'm lost for words,' Penelope said, plopping herself down at the table. 'How unfortunate for us all that my husband is besotted with you, you with your husband and your husband with another.'

'I only intended to make him jealous, in the hope of winning him back. I thought that if he saw how attractive I was to other men, he might want me again, the way he used to. If not Nicholas, it would have been someone else. I'm sorry Penelope. I really am. You probably think I'm pathetic.'

'No.' She shook her head. She should have been feeling complacent, but she wasn't. All she felt was pity.

'I expect they'll be wondering where we've got to,' Amanda said tearfully.

'I expect they will. Let them wonder.'

NO DIVING

She never forgot the day she took her first dive in the local municipal baths, presided over by a plump, officious woman who constantly barked orders and blew endlessly on a tin whistle. She remembered how she lay awake the night before, praying for an intervention, longing for a reprieve.

The next day, resigned to her fate and stricken with terror, she stood at the edge of the pool, gazing into the murky water, her tormentor close by, eager to inflict a punishment for which she had committed no crime. She closed her eyes, took a deep breath and at the ear-splitting blast of the whistle, dived in.

Vietato Tuffarsi. NO DIVING. It was written in bold red letters at either end of the swimming pool, high on a cliff top that looked out over the Mediterranean Sea. How the words evoked in them a wellspring of memories as she glided along in the still air, breathing in the heady aroma of orange blossom and the exotic scent of tanning oil each time a light breeze came wafting her way. One more length, just one more and then a light lunch on the terrace.

She waited until the bronzed attendant, with the smouldering looks of an Adonis, turned his back. Then she climbed the steps furtively, even though she was certain his interest lay elsewhere, his dark brown eyes carefully trained on the lithe young beauties strutting self-consciously around the pool, eagerly vying for attention. How old she felt and how envious of their youth, so that every strain of their infectious laughter filled her with unwelcome indignation.

Having no desire to sit among the other guests, who converged daily to compare indulgences and mull over petty vexations, she positioned herself near the far end of the pool, in the shade of the orange blossom tree, where she read short stories and dozed until noon.

Lunch on the terrace had a deliberate air of stylish informality, tablecloths woven from soft linen and flecked with random knots of imperfection, crockery hand-painted by local craftsmen in bold splashes of red and yellow, and the glassware a cool aqua blue, all so resonant of Mediterranean life. The staff called her Signora and pandered to her with a benevolence reserved for dotage.

She had a liking for grilled fish and salad, but each day listened patiently while Luigi, the zealous young waiter, recited the specials in his best English accent, then handed her the menu, which she faithfully perused. Anything Signora desires.

One morning, on her way to the forecourt, where the shuttle bus took guests into town, she noticed a tall pale-skinned man walking briskly across the terrace. His face was partially obscured by a wide-brimmed Panama hat, although instinct told her they were of a similar age.

Something about him piqued her curiosity; the hat perhaps, or the way he moved so purposefully, with the impressive agility of an athlete.

'Mi scusi Luigi...'

'Signora?' Luigi replied, scurrying towards her with unaffected enthusiasm.

'Tell me, the gentleman over there...' she raised her finger and pointed discreetly, 'Is he alone?'

'Si Signora, alone, arreev-ah this morning. English. Very good, yes?'

'Yes yes. Thank you. Grazie Luigi.'

She took the bus into town and spent the morning wandering around, browsing in gift shops at cheap-looking souvenirs and sidestepping eager shopkeepers competing for business with their 'lovely lady' banter. Still, she revelled in it all, the hustle and bustle, the smells, the sounds, the colours, so vibrant and life affirming, and for a moment she felt young again.

She stopped to buy gelato and sat on a nearby wall watching the hordes of tourists idle by, sunburnt and spent from the relentless heat. And she thought of him, the tall man.

In the afternoon, when she returned to the hotel, she couldn't help but look out for him, by the pool and among the winding terraces of lemon groves that seemed to spiral to the heavens, but it wasn't until much later that she caught sight of him. He was strolling blithely through the lobby, waving at staff with the air of a local dignitary.

He sat at an empty table on the terrace, took off his hat and placed it ceremoniously on the chair beside him, at the same time summoning the waiter with his other hand. In the evening light his face had a pleasing countenance, encouraged perhaps by the small candle glowing in a crimson glass bowl, and although they had not yet spoken, his presence had cheered her, had lifted her spirits.

The next day, as she dozed in the sultry heat of late morning, she heard the distant voice of an Englishman. It grew gradually louder and when she looked up, she saw the bronzed Adonis escorting the tall man to a sun lounger in the shade of a large umbrella. He had removed his hat and she could see him much clearer now, but although he was not exactly unappealing, the immediate spark of attraction was more or less absent. She had seesawed between the faint hope of romance and the fear of it, more than once telling herself it was only friendship she sought now, an easy companionship, pure and unfettered by the gnawing complexities of the heart.

He was still sitting by the pool at sunset, his face buried in a book. As she stood to leave he looked up and acknowledged her with a smile, so she decided to approach him.

'Excuse me,' she said.

He placed a postcard on the open page, closed the book and gave her a look that suggested he had been expecting her.

'Hi. I've um…I've seen you around and I thought I'd introduce myself, as we seem to be among the few guests of, well, of another generation, if you don't mind me saying.'

'Why would I mind?' he replied, apparently unruffled by her words.

'Anyway, I was wondering if you'd like to join me for a drink on the terrace this evening, unless of course you have company,' she said.

'Well, it just so happens I'm free, so yes, that would be very nice,' he said and smiled broadly to assuage her anxiety.

'Great. Shall we say seven?'

'Seven it is.'

When she returned to her room, she took a dress from the wardrobe and hung it over the door in readiness. Catching a glimpse of herself in the long mirror, in the unflattering semi-light of the hour, she suddenly felt foolish, wondering if it might be pity that had compelled him to accept, but any doubt soon gave way to a small flutter of excitement and it was then she realised she didn't even know his name.

When she arrived on the terrace that evening he was waiting for her, looking out to sea like a character in a historical drama, his tall silhouette adding to the illusion.

'Good evening,' she said, with a chirpiness that disguised her jitters.

He turned around slowly.

'Good evening. You look enchanting!' The words tripped too easily off his tongue, but she thanked him all the same.

'Philip. Pleased to meet you,' he said extending a hand.

'Valerie,' she replied, taking it.

They stood for a while in silence, watching the twinkling lights of a yacht in the distance and the rolling waves gently lapping the shoreline in the inky-darkness of evening.

Luigi escorted them to a small table by the stone steps that led to the beach. In the centre was a tall ivory candle, flickering steadily in the night air.

'I've been wondering to myself why a lady like you would be travelling alone,' Philip said, the timbre of his voice conveying a hint of suspicion.

'Well, I enjoy travelling alone. I like having the freedom to do exactly as I please when I please,' Valerie replied, almost defensively.

'Nevertheless, you're very brave.'

'Oh, I wouldn't say that.'

'How so?'

'Well, I'll give you an example of real courage. Something happened to me many years ago that has been on my mind since I arrived.' She fell silent for a moment.

'Sounds intriguing,' he said.

'I was young and shy,' she started. 'I suppose you could say I was the timid girl in school. Anyway, every week the whole class was packed off to the local baths for swimming lessons. Then one day we learned to dive. I can still remember it now, every moment, like it was yesterday. I was petrified, numb with fear, as this dreadful ogre of a woman stood by, a large tin whistle pressed firmly to her lips. But then an extraordinary thing happened, as if the gods were on my side. She blew hard on the whistle and as I dived into the water, the fear drained out of me and I suddenly felt like the bravest girl in the world.'

'And now, do you still dive?'

'Oh no, I don't have that kind of courage anymore. I guess that's what the years do. They strip us of the spirit of our youth.'

'Why so defeatist? We'll have you diving again in no time,' he said, wagging his finger decisively.

'Ah, then you haven't seen the signs. No Diving. So you see, even if I wanted to, I couldn't possibly,' she said with a great sigh of relief.

'Oh, forget about that. Rules are made to be broken.'

'Perhaps. Anyway, what brings you here?'

'Mine is a long story, one that I won't trouble you with on such a lovely evening,' he said.

'Please, I'd like to hear your story.'

He stared into his lap.

'Well then, here it is. About a year ago, in fact almost to the day, I lost my job at an auction house in London. Something about a reshuffle and changing times. I suppose they considered me a bit of a relic. So it was thank you very much and goodbye. I suppose if I'm honest, I knew it was coming. All the signs were there, but thirty years, just like that?' He snapped his fingers and looked at her glumly.

'What did you do then?' she asked in a sympathetic voice.

'I sat around moping for a while, feeling sorry for myself. Then, having tired of that, I began to put the feelers out, called on a few of the old contacts, but after months of nothing doing, I quit. If I'm honest, it was a bit of a blow to my already wounded ego. Fortunately, I happen to be solvent and although I'm no millionaire, I no longer have to work. They say everyone has a book in them, so, one morning I got up, sat at my desk and started writing.'

'Good for you.'

'At first I just sat there, staring at a blank screen, but before I knew it, I had the beginnings of a story. That was six months ago and now, here I am, still writing. It doesn't as yet have an ending. That's the hard part.'

'How interesting. So you're here for inspiration?'

'Yes I suppose I am...in a way.'

'What's it about, your story?'

'Well, oddly enough dear Valerie, it's about courage.'

'Courage to do what?'

'To do whatever you want. To live life, to confront your fears.'

'Like diving you mean.'

'Exactly. Like diving.'

They talked late into evening, until the candle petered out.

The next morning Philip was waiting for her at breakfast, beckoning her over.

'Good morning,' he said, his hand gesturing to the empty seat beside him.

'Good morning,' Valerie said rather timorously, as if she had been guilty of a minor indiscretion.

'Today I feel inspired! How about you? Feeling courageous?'

'Well, if you mean what I think you mean, then no, I'm not.'

'We'll see,' he said with a mischievous grin.

After breakfast they sat together by the pool and she felt as though all eyes were on them, especially those of the smug young girls, who seemed to scoff at anyone over the age of twenty, with the exception of the bronzed Adonis, who must have been all of twenty-two. When Philip eyed them up and down, brazen and unapologetic, she felt a sudden pang of jealousy. She thought of how he might have fallen for her had he known her long ago, in all her youthful beauty, when men pursued her at every turn. She watched him as his eyes settled on a girl sitting by the edge of the pool, splashing water with her brightly painted toes and leaning in seductively, baring just enough with which to awaken his desire. He seemed hypnotised by her, with her long sun-bleached hair, golden-brown skin and pouting, shimmery lips. She pretended not to notice him, or the several other men ogling her as they shifted uneasily on their sunbeds. Valerie took a few deep breaths before tiptoeing gingerly to the pool. On the odd occasion that his eyes met hers, she smiled, careful not to reveal her disenchantment. She swam a few lengths, then stopped to look out over the ocean that glistened like a million jewels, as the speedboats bounced and skimmed the surface, accompanied by the terrified shrieks of delight echoing in the salty air.

When she returned to his side, his interest had moved to another girl who was sitting nearby, blending big dollops of thick white cream into her pale young skin with the deftness of a siren. Valerie watched hopelessly as the young girl taunted the men with every stroke of her soft flesh.

'She's a bit out of your league isn't she?' Valerie said, unable to contain her resentment now.

'I'm sorry?' Philip said and frowned, clearly thrown by her remark.

'They prefer someone their own age, like Adonis over there.' She nodded in the direction of the attendant and laughed nervously, in the hope of undoing his obvious displeasure.

'One can but dream,' he said raising an eyebrow.

'I suppose so. After all, who would be interested in someone like me?'

'Come now, don't be so down on yourself. You're a fine looking woman.'

She should have been feeling flattered, but she wasn't. The night before he had told her she looked enchanting, but now, surrounded by so much youth and beauty, 'a fine looking woman' didn't quite cut the mustard.

They hardly spoke for the rest of the day, not least because her words had brought about an awkwardness between them and she regretted having uttered them.

'Will I see you tonight?' she said hesitantly as she rose to leave.

'Would you like to?' His voice was stern, almost punishing.

'Yes.'

'Well, it's a date then. Seven thirty.'

As she walked away, she felt a knot of fear in the pit of her stomach, just as she had when she took her first dive all those years ago.

She felt sure that the awkwardness of the afternoon would persist into evening, but when he came striding towards her, his arms open as though greeting an old friend, she knew it had passed.

'She's here!' he said pressing his hands to his chest with the affectation of a tormented actor and she laughed, more from a sense of relief than anything else. The knot loosened, but still she felt foolish and far more unsettling than that, she now felt vulnerable. She had mistakenly let her guard down, allowed her feelings to get the better of her. Perhaps it was the candlelight, or the wine, that had unexpectedly thrown her emotions off kilter. Maybe the dependable spark of days gone by had manifested itself in other, more subtle ways, no longer the barometer by which she had measured desire.

For most of the evening and for the first time since they met, he talked about his past, the good times and the bad, but not once did he mention if there had been a wife.

'Stop me if I'm being intrusive,' she said, a perceptible tremble in her voice, 'but have you ever been married?'

'Married? Nooooo!' he said shaking his head emphatically. 'Why, do I look like the marrying kind?'

'I don't know. I'm not sure what the marrying kind looks like, having never been married myself.'

'Ah, so we have something in common,' he replied.

'Yes, except I would have liked to have married and had a child, maybe two.'

'And that's where we differ. I won't deny that there have been a number of women in my life, but when I told them I had no interest in fathering a child, they upped and left, said they couldn't afford to waste their valuable, fertile years with a man with whom there was no future. So you see, I seem to have had an uncanny knack of attracting the maternal kind.'

'I thought most women were the maternal kind,' she said. 'It's not that I wasn't myself, but I try to be philosophical. If it was meant to be...' She looked off into the distance and for a few minutes they sat in silence, although it seemed to her much longer.

'Ah, I see swordfish is the special this evening,' Philip said, summoning Luigi.

After dinner they lingered on the terrace. It was Thursday, the night the pianist from the nearby town came to play and take requests from love-struck honeymooners. He wore pink trousers with a matching tailcoat, beige satin shirt and a beige straw hat trimmed with pink ribbon. The guests looked at one another and sniggered behind cupped hands at his comical appearance and exaggerated, faraway smile, as he idly played a few choice melodies to set the mood.

'Do you know Can't Take My Eyes Off You?' asked a young woman, raising her hand coyly.

'Anything for you Senora!' he replied, enlivened at the chance to flaunt his skills and garner much-craved attention. He went over to her and they exchanged a few words, then he sashayed back to the piano, flicking the tail of his coat as he sat.

'Theece one is for Daniel and Samantha,' he announced. A few people applauded as the newlyweds, struck by a fit of giggles, made their way to the empty space on the terrace that doubled as a dance floor, and waited for the music to begin.

'You jast aah good to be true...' he sang as they laughed some more and gazed longingly into one another's eyes.

'They look lovely don't they?' Valerie said.

'Yes, I suppose they do.'

'Their whole lives in front of them and most of ours behind us.'

'That's a pessimistic view, isn't it?'

'Is it? Oh, I didn't mean it to be. What I meant was...'

'Yes, I know what you meant, but you're alive and well and having a bloody good time in this gorgeous hotel on this beautiful island, in the sparkling company of yours truly. What's to be down about?' he said, tilting his chair back and locking his fingers together behind his head. 'It's the natural order of things and you just have to accept it.'

'Sorry. It must be the wine talking.'

By the time the pianist had finished playing, there were only a few people left on the terrace and the waiter, ever jolly, hovered until Philip escorted Valerie back to her room.

'Well, goodnight.' He took her hand and kissed it.

'Goodnight...and thank you for a lovely evening,' she said.

When she closed the door, an awful feeling of loneliness washed over her, more than if she had never met him.

'Today's the day!' Philip declared the following morning, while young Adonis opened sun loungers and whistled cheerfully.

'For?' Valerie asked, even though she knew exactly what he meant.

'We'll take it slow, no hurry. What do you say we jump in the deep end a few times first, just to get used to it.'

'Jump!' she exclaimed. 'Jump? No, I don't think so.'

'We'll do it together.'

Apart from the kiss on the hand, there had been no physical contact between them, even during the candlelit setting of dinner. He hadn't slid his fingers surreptitiously across the table to meet hers, nor had he squeezed her arm, stroked her hair or placed his hand around her waist when they strolled together.

'Okay,' she said reluctantly, 'but promise you'll stay with me.'

She felt like a little girl again, that same petrified little girl of long ago. She looked into his eyes. He smiled and nodded.

They walked to the deep end of the pool and stood side by side.

'Deep breaths,' he said, 'take a few deep breaths and be calm.'

She took a couple of steps back.

'No. I can't jump. I can't do it. Sorry.'

'Of course you can. There's nothing to it. Here, take my hand.' She put her hand in his and tightened her grip as they stepped forward together. When she looked around, she had assumed all eyes would be on them but, mercifully, they weren't. The young girls were too busy watching Adonis, whispering and giggling each time they caught his eye, while others dozed or read and honeymooners canoodled.

'Okay, one two three jump!'

'Today, Luigi, I'll have a glass of champagne with my lunch. I'm celebrating.'

'Si Signora!' Luigi replied with his usual unbridled devotion.

Valerie sipped on her champagne, savouring every drop as she relived it over and again; her fear, Philip holding her hand and then the jump itself. She felt elated, maybe because she knew that this wasn't just about being brave. It was so much more than that.

'When I popped into town this afternoon, I went on a mission of sorts,' Philip said that evening at dinner.

'Oh?' Valerie replied, a quizzical but happy look on her face.

'I wanted to buy you a gift, something to spur you on to the next challenge.'

He reached into his shirt pocket and took out a small silk purse, which he placed in the palm of her hand.

'Open it,' he said.

'What is it?'

'Open it and you'll see.'

It was a porcelain brooch in the shape of a lady with scarlet lips, wearing a turquoise swimsuit and poised to dive.

'It's beautiful. I don't know what to say, except thank you. Thank you!' Her eyes welled up with emotion.

'Think of it as a small enticement,' he said, stroking her cheek with a surprising tenderness and at that moment, she knew she would dive again, not only for courage, but also for him.

THE PENDULUM

It was five years since William had gone, but it seemed like only yesterday, for he was constantly in Hermione's thoughts, from the moment she opened her eyes in the morning until the drowsing seconds before sleep. She sometimes dreamed about him, always the same dream. As in life, they would be bartering over some worthless artefact in a crowded foreign market and it was then they were at their happiest.

Hermione had been careful to preserve things exactly as they were on that fateful day. A firm believer in orderliness, William frequently extolled on the virtues of having a place for everything and everything in its place. It had become his mantra and with him gone, Hermione felt honour-bound to make it hers. They were kindred spirits, she and William. In truth, they had amassed an inordinate amount of keepsakes that she no longer had a need for and yet couldn't bring herself to part with, for everything, down to the simplest ornament, had acquired its own unique narrative.

Long ago and in a moment of sentimentality they made a pact. Every time they came upon something new – for instance, the Corinthian-style vase they brought back from Crete – they gave it a story, so that whenever they looked at it, they could summon the appropriate reminiscence, until eventually every room in the house resonated with recollections of times past. Such was the extent of William's dedication, he catalogued every piece by item and room and although each was in its own way compelling, for Hermione only one was truly extraordinary.

To look at, one would never have guessed at its import, for the pendulum was no more pleasing to the eye than anything else in the house and only by exploring its potential could its true efficacy be revealed.

Hermione had first seen it in a shop window many years earlier, one afternoon in spring. She and William had gone for a drive in the country and, after a generous pub lunch, strolled into the local town. William stopped to rest on a bench in the square, while Hermione went for a wander. It was then that she saw it, the cut of the crystal mesmerising in its dazzling incandescence as it twirled this way and that. Suddenly the sun struck it, throwing a magnificent beam of light in William's direction, illuminating his whole face. Convinced it was an omen, Hermione bought it there and then.

As chance would have it, on a visit to the library several weeks earlier, she overheard two women in the neighbouring aisle, discussing a book that one of them had recently borrowed. The book in question eulogised on the benefits of pendulum dowsing, something quite foreign to Hermione. The woman went on in some detail, saying how she had been unable to put it down, and as her voice diminished to a barely audible whisper, the furtive manner in which she spoke, despite the mandatory hush of the library, aroused Hermione's curiosity. She waited until they left, thumbing through books that held no interest for her, before going in search of the book the unseen woman had spoken of. She took it from the shelf, opened it surreptitiously and began to read - *Pendulum dowsing can be used to establish unity between people, places and things. A pendulum can be useful in finding missing objects and may also be able to predict the future* – so that by the time she chanced on it several weeks later, she was already well acquainted with its supposed powers.

Although a lover of beautiful and intriguing things, William was rather a cynic when it came to anything bordering on the abstruse, never having been one to stray outside the familiar confines of practicality, and so, as much as he deemed the pendulum not entirely uninteresting to look at, it held no deeper fascination for him.

The first time Hermione was to witness its powers was one evening when, alone in the house, she decided to put it to the test. A few days earlier she had mislaid a gold necklace and had been anxious about it ever since, as it was the one that William had bought her on their twentieth wedding anniversary. She had worn it to the monthly bridge meeting as usual, but the next morning discovered it missing. She hadn't told him about it, knowing his disdain for carelessness, but instead searched high and low in the hope of retrieving it, before he noticed it was gone.

She sat at the kitchen table, took a few deep breaths and held the pendulum in front of her as steadily as she could. She wasn't sure what to ask of it. Was the necklace lost for good? The pendulum swung in an anti-clockwise direction, indicating that no, it was not. She breathed a sigh of relief, then asked if it was in the house. It swung, rapidly, clockwise, indicating that yes, it was. She was trembling, her excitement palpable. Could it be in the bedroom? No was the swift response. Perhaps it was in the bathroom. She was forever leaving her jewellery in the bathroom. Once again, the answer was no. She hesitated for a moment, but fearing her hesitation would give way to doubt, quickly moved on to the next question. What about the kitchen? Is it here? You must tell me! She was pleading now, desperate for an answer. The pendulum swung furiously in a clockwise direction, in an ever-widening spiral. She dropped it on the table and raced around the kitchen in search of the necklace, until at last she came upon it in the cupboard above the sink and it was then that she remembered having put it there for cleaning the night she returned from the bridge meeting. She shrieked with joy and amazement at the pendulum's astonishing accuracy and thought of the many other things about which she could interrogate it.

In the years that followed it became her soothsayer and she consulted it at every turn of her life. Even in the light of its extraordinary precision, which William would often bear witness to, he continued to dismiss it as utter nonsense.

During the months prior to his death, Hermione had taken to questioning the pendulum on a daily basis, asking trivial questions of it, such as whether to cook fish or beef for dinner, while William looked on, perpetually bemused by her ever-increasing obsession.

One evening, they were getting ready to visit a friend who lived about a mile away. William had taken his car to the garage for repair the previous morning, so they decided to walk, but as they were about to leave, there was a sudden torrential downpour. Reluctant to brave the weather, Hermione suggested consulting the pendulum. William wouldn't hear of it and insisted they go as planned, but she was adamant and could not be dissuaded. She sat at the kitchen table, pendulum in hand, ready to receive its wisdom. She asked if the downpour would soon cease. No was the answer. She looked out of the window and watched the rain thrashing against it with such force as she had never seen before. Will the wind soon abate? No. Is it wise to leave the house? For a moment the pendulum hung, motionless, in the air, then began rotating in a clockwise direction. She wondered if her reluctance to leave had somehow influenced the pendulum's swing. She called upstairs to William as he was getting ready, imploring him not to go. He came down, an unequivocal look of despair etched upon his face. He shook his head, put on his raincoat, removed his umbrella from the stand and certain now that Hermione would not be accompanying him, left alone.

Outside on the rain-battered street, William raced hurriedly along, the relentless assault of the wind propelling him ever closer to his destination. As he fought to keep a steady hold on the umbrella, a constant stream of cars washed the pavement with miniature tidal waves and he thought of poor Hermione, downcast and defeated, sitting in the warmth of the kitchen in the ever-familiar throes of divination. Suddenly, he felt an overwhelming urge to turn back.

He began running in the direction of home, as if carried by an inexplicable force, all the while battling with the oncoming rain that bore into his face like a million tiny needles. He thought of what he would say to her when he walked through the door, of how sorry he was for doubting her. He would put his arms around her and comfort her and everything would be fine.

As he arrived at the corner of their street, the rain still lashing at his face, an enormous gust of wind swept him without warning into the main road and the oncoming traffic. A large truck swerved as it took the bend, before letting out a deafening screech and in an instant William was gone, his body shattered and lifeless by the side of the kerb.

Hermione sits alone most evenings, only the pendulum for company now. She thinks of what could have been, of the places she and William had yet to discover, places they had only seen in the guidebooks. She longs for his company once more, the aching sense of emptiness ubiquitous.

If only he had shared her unwavering faith in the extraordinary powers of the pendulum.

THE MERITS OF DARJEELING

Nothing appealed to Melissa Merryweather more than a nice, refreshing cup of tea. She often bragged that tea ran through her veins and swore that by simply flaring her nostrils and breathing in the warm vapour, she could immediately identify almost every kind of tea, be it black, white or green. But of all the teas she had enjoyed, none was a match for her beloved Darjeeling, the Champagne of teas, of which she claimed a knowledge unsurpassed, not that she had much competition. It seemed everyone drank coffee these days - espresso, cappuccino, skinny latte - whatever that was - and a multitude of others she had never heard of. For Melissa, tea was a far more civilised affair, one that simply cried out for the company of a warm scone, with generous helpings of jam and clotted cream. The trouble was, she had not a single friend who shared her passion for the much-revered leaf. And so, once a month, which was all her budget would allow, she took herself off, alone, to Dewberry's, a rather grand tea room in the centre of town, the last of its kind, where the vestiges of old money frequently converged and where she was afforded the kind of service otherwise reserved for royalty.

Melissa always sat at the same table in the middle of the room, facing the revolving door, where she could see all the comings and goings and, more importantly, the comings and goings could see her. Friday afternoons were best, because that was when old Madame Leboeuf played the harp. It wasn't her real name of course, but it sounded so refined, so European. Melissa had become friendly with Lulu the waitress and as a consequence (thanks to an inquisitive nature equalled only by her own), had learned that Madame originally hailed from Skegness and that her real name was in fact Marjorie Pickles. How fortunate Melissa was to have been blessed with such a fragrant name that tripped off the tongue with the daintiness of a nymph.

Although she had seen the menu countless times, Melissa studied it with childlike anticipation. So many teas to choose from, pastries to make the mouth water and, if she was feeling a little reckless, a glass of bubbly, to add some sparkle to the occasion. Melissa loved occasions, perhaps because she had been invited to so few.

She would have liked to share the afternoon with a companion, a fellow enthusiast, or anybody for that matter, would have loved to discuss the subtle delicacies and merits of the various teas, not to mention the delicious pastries. But it was not to be, and as much as she was at ease in her own company - indeed, prided herself on the fact of her fortitude - now and then she felt the cold hand of loneliness tap her on the shoulder, a poignant reminder of her abiding solitude, and it was then that she rued the lure of the Moët, which invariably induced a mild inebriation, dampened her spirits and made her more than a touch maudlin. Nevertheless, she lived for her monthly teas, counted the days and then the hours, the ritual, the splendour of it all, as if for the last time.

One Friday afternoon, she noticed a man who had been causing quite a stir at the front desk. He was tall, with imposing features, and although his expression was that of a malcontent, he was not entirely displeasing to the eye. In one hand he held a shiny black cane, on which he leant, while gesticulating to the frazzled young hostess with the other. Melissa called Lulu over to find out what all the fuss was about. It seemed he was insisting on a table, even though every one was occupied. He hadn't booked - an absolute must on a Friday - and was clearly vexed to be told that none were free for some time. It had occurred to Melissa to invite him to share hers, which could comfortably accommodate two, but, discouraged by his brusque manner, she said nothing. Then fate intervened. He began marching in her direction, tapping his cane purposefully on the parquet floor, so that everyone turned to look at him, even though, cane or not, a man of his loftiness wouldn't have gone unnoticed.

'May I,' he said pointing the cane at the empty chair.

'Well, I...'

'Don't worry dear lady, I won't trouble you for conversation,' he said, as he sat down, raised his hand and beckoned Lulu over with a wag of his index finger.

'A pot of your finest Darjeeling,' he demanded.

'Yes sir,' Lulu said, winking furtively at Melissa.

'You've made a good choice,' Melissa said, in an effort to dispel any unpleasantness.

'Good choice?' he asked, a look of mild irritation on his face.

'Yes, the Darjeeling. I rarely drink anything else, although all the teas here are exceptional.'

'Is that so?'

'Oh yes!'

'Then, if, as you say, they are all exceptional, isn't it time you tried something else?' he said, smirking.

'But Darjeeling is my personal favourite,' Melissa replied, with the touching enthusiasm of a child.

'What an uninteresting life you lead, dear woman,' he said, causing her to recoil, her eyes widening to convey her dismay.

'Don't you think that was rather uncalled for? I'm simply trying to be friendly,' she said, defying his arrogance and pouring herself a cup of tea.

'I speak as I find,' he said, jerking his head back abruptly, his long thin nose cutting the air like a knife.

'So it seems.'

The thought of having to sit opposite this decidedly unpleasant man began to fill her with dread, the one day in the month that she so looked forward to now being denied her.

They sat in silence and she watched him empty the teapot, his eyes constantly scanning the room with an air of grandeur. Presently, and much to Melissa's relief, Madame Leboeuf entered to a polite ripple of applause. She had the look of someone from a bygone era – the faded blue satin gown, the corsage waistband, the ruby

40

lips and lacquered coiffure all contributing to a somewhat whimsical appearance. She swished across the room to the far corner, where a swathe of red velvet hung over a dressing screen that served as a backdrop. She smiled and bowed several times, acknowledging various tables in the room, then swept the stool with her hand, sat, arranged her dress and began to play.

'You women all go in for this airy-fairy claptrap,' he said.

'Well if you find it so unpleasant, why don't you just...sod off?' Melissa replied with an uncustomary boldness that she, surprisingly, relished.

'Because it's the only place I can get a decent cup of tea dear woman,' he said, unperturbed.

'They sell it in the tea shop by the entrance, so might I suggest you buy some on your way out and drink it at home, where you won't be bothered by airy-fairy claptrap!'

'My my, you're a feisty woman. I do love a woman with a bit of oomph,' he said rubbing his hands together with glee, his cheeks steadily reddening. No one had ever described her as feisty before and to her surprise, she quite liked it. She was an ordinary woman, plain by her own admission, a woman whose emotions had seldom been stirred, if indeed at all, but now this pompous boor of a man was teasing her, preying on her vulnerability, a vulnerability she thought she had concealed behind a veil of fearlessness and she suddenly found herself both attracted to and irritated by him in equal measure.

Over in the corner, Madame Leboeuf was furiously plucking on the harp; a rousing soundtrack to their contretemps.

'The old girl's going like the clappers today,' he said laughing.

'I think she's rather good. Besides, she's popular with the customers,' Melissa replied and he could see, by the wounded look on her face, that he had gone too far.

'Forgive me,' he said, his hand reaching across the table and resting lightly on her arm. 'I didn't mean to tease you, but I'm afraid you strike me as someone who is very teasable.'

'Yes,' Melissa replied, 'I suppose I am.'

'Do you come here every week?' he asked, the flush in his cheeks subsiding now.

'Oh no, that would be far too extravagant. Just the once a month,' she said, gazing dolefully into her tea cup.

'There's no shame in spoiling oneself,' he said.

'And you,' she asked, 'how often do you come here?'

'Occasionally, when I find myself in town and in need of a good cup of tea,' he said and smiled.

'But you don't book,' she replied.

'No. I'm the impulsive kind. For instance, had I booked this afternoon, I would certainly not have made your acquaintance. But, perhaps you'd have preferred it that way.'

'To be honest, it's nice to have some company.'

'I must say, as much as I am not averse to the company of others, I am quite happy in my own,' he said smugly.

'I expect that's because it's by choice and not necessity,' she replied.

They talked a while longer and now and then Melissa looked around, in the hope of being seen by a few of the regulars.

'Well, I'm afraid I must go,' he announced, glancing at his watch. He picked up his cane, stood, nodded and made for the exit, like someone who had a train to catch.

A wave of disappointment swept over her and she felt a strong compulsion to call after him, to ask if or when she might see him again, but her reserve was quickly restored. He paid his bill, exchanged a few words with the hostess and turned to look at Melissa, who was watching him intently. He smiled and raised a hand, before disappearing through the revolving door and out of sight.

Madame Leboeuf stopped playing and rose from her seat to take a bow, accompanied by another mild, but contented, ripple of applause. Melissa looked around the bustling room, as people filled their mouths with pastries and laughed raucously, and for a moment, she felt as if they were laughing at her. She poured herself another cup of tea, thoughts of him whirring about inside her head. Their meeting had been so brief and yet, in spite of him, his unnerving presence had aroused something in her, had awakened feelings she didn't know she possessed, and informed her of her loneliness more than she could have imagined. She took a handkerchief from her handbag and wiped away a tear from the corner of her eye.

'Are you okay Miss Merryweather?' Lulu said.

'Oh...yes, I'm fine thank you Lulu,' Melissa replied, sniffling into the handkerchief.

'An interesting man, rather fascinating I'd say,' Lulu said, raising an eyebrow.

'Yes, he is indeed,' Melissa replied, dabbing the handkerchief under her nose.

'Can I get you anything else?' Lulu asked, her eyes scouring the tables for empty cups and plates.

'No, thank you. Just my bill please.'

'Not necessary,' Lulu said shaking her head.

'What do you mean?' Melissa asked, a quizzical look on her face.

'The gentleman has already paid,' Lulu replied, smiling.

'Already paid? But, why?'

'He insisted. Said something about teasing you. Oh, and he left this note.' She handed her a small sheet of folded paper, which she opened and read to herself – *Dear Lady, please allow me to make up for my impertinence. I shall be here at the same time next Friday and would be most pleased if you will share my table. We have much to discuss on the merits of Darjeeling. Sincerely yours, Julian Drinkwater.*

Melissa felt an unfamiliar rush of pleasure sweep through her as she strained the last drops of Darjeeling from the pot.

BURLESQUE

After endless deliberation and not a few nights of sleepless consternation, she had finally settled on a stage name. Lady Narcisse. It went with the territory and was rather more exotic than Brenda Green, a name that did little to allude to the glamorous world of burlesque.

She had dreamed of being a ballet dancer, but grew too tall and ended up working as an insurance clerk in a dingy office in Moorgate. It's not how she'd planned things.

In the hope of better acquainting herself with the nocturnal fraternity, she took a job as a cloakroom attendant in a nightclub and although the tips were good, she soon twigged that the confines of a coat closet in a dimly lit lobby were not the route to success.

The day job was a doddle. She could do it with her eyes closed, which left her free to while away the hours fantasising about feathers, sequins and tassels. She must have seen *Gypsy* a hundred times, knew every scene inside out. Night after night she practised in her bedroom, determined to stop at nothing in order to realise her dream. She spent her holiday pay on outfits from a shop in Shaftesbury Avenue that a friend of her mother's had seen advertised in Am-Dram Quarterly.

There had been a boyfriend once, long ago. His name was Derek and she would occasionally try out the new routines on him, but he was somewhat of a prude and didn't share her enthusiasm for exotic dance, all-consumed as he was with a passion for fly fishing. Needless to say, the liaison was short lived and in any case, she couldn't be doing with that sort of thing once she hit the big time. Burlesque and fly fishing did not make for good bedfellows.

Her bedroom was her sanctuary, her little palace of opulence, shut off from the dreary world outside, where each evening she played her part, where once more she became *The Delectable Lady Narcisse*, her thin lips stained blood red and pursed with the promise of seduction. Lady Narcisse, object of the adoring masses, the roar of adulation broken only by the familiar sound of her mother's voice beckoning her downstairs for a nightcap of cocoa and shortbread.

She had read somewhere that burlesque was making a comeback stateside, in New York City, where dreams were made. Perhaps her talents would be best nurtured there, among the neon lights and iconic yellow taxis that glimmered in the sultry, intoxicating night air. Then there was her accent. She'd heard that they were mad for the English accent. She had also heard, though she couldn't say where, that discerning Manhattan gentlemen favoured the more mature, curvaceous woman, such as she.

New York was calling. She could feel it in her bones.

She set about making plans. She would have to give notice at the office, say her farewells and listen to the naysayers, telling her how she was making a big mistake and reminding her what a cushy number she had, not to mention lunch in the pub on Fridays.

There was much else to be done, not least the matter of breaking the news to her mother, who would surely understand. After all, she knew all there was to know about hopes and dreams, having herself once aspired to a life on the stage, before it had been cruelly thwarted by love.

'Ladies and Gentleman, may I have your attention please. Tonight, and for your eyes only, all the way from London Town England, New York City gives you the one…the only…*The Delectable Lady Narciiiiiisse*!'

The crowd roared their applause as she strutted seductively, swaggering onto the stage, fuelled by a sea of silhouettes, heads bobbing in the darkness, their frenzied hoots and howls unbridled.

Lady stood centre stage, drinking in every last drop of the dream, jubilant and breathless with excitement. She closed her eyes and for a moment, it seemed so real she could almost taste it.

She sat at the dressing table and stared into the mirror, downcast and spent, the lines on her face streaked with black mascara. She slowly removed her make-up, until every trace of Lady was gone. Quietly sobbing, she unzipped her dress. A few feathers flew this way and that as it fell to the floor in a crumpled heap. She stepped out of it, picked it up carefully, smoothed the creases with her hand and hung it on a pink satin hanger, on which she had, during the lonely nights, painstakingly embroidered her stage name. She put on her pyjamas and set out her clothes for the morning. Monday was always the busiest day in the office.

'Brenda! Brenda! Hurry up. Your cocoa's getting cold.'

A GLASS OF CHAMPAGNE

Magda Hamilton was a woman of simple tastes, untainted by ambition or desire. Her husband Joseph, a bookkeeper in a large construction company, was similarly ordained, cut from the same unremarkable cloth. They had few friends, seldom socialised and were at their most contented in each other's company, so that there existed between them a sort of smugness, as though they were the custodians of a great secret.

One morning Joseph arrived at the office to find an envelope on his desk. This in itself was not unusual. He was used to the familiar sight of dull manila circulars piling up in his in-tray, waiting to be processed. But this was not one of those. It was instead a cream-coloured envelope of the finest quality, addressed in gold lettering and marked 'Personal'. He ran his fingers over it, almost mesmerised, excited at seeing his name so elegantly penned with the sweep of a calligrapher's hand. He opened it carefully, slowly removed the card inside and read it in a hushed voice – 'Mr and Mrs Joseph Hamilton are Cordially Invited to Celebrate the 10th Wedding Anniversary of Mr and Mrs Albert Edelson. RSVP...'

Mr Edelson, Joseph's boss, was a surly man, whose generosity, in spite of his character, could not be faulted, a man frequently feted for his philanthropy and, as a consequence, prey to more than a few opportunists, his wife among them. Those who knew him well put his boorishness down to her bullying, which he tolerated for reasons that were obvious to all. Mrs Edelson was a beautiful creature, many years his junior, his 'trophy wife' as the girls in the office sneeringly called her. In fact, such was his devotion that he rarely curbed her proclivity for reckless spending and quietly overlooked her occasional indiscretions. What he did not know was that Mrs Edelson, a woman of humble beginnings, was herself plagued by insecurity, guarding her position and fending off female adversaries with a fortitude that could challenge a battalion.

When Joseph returned home that evening, without stopping to remove his coat, he marched straight into the kitchen, where Magda was chopping vegetables and humming along to the radio. He held the invitation out in front of her. She looked at him quizzically, wiped her hands on the front of her apron and took it from him. She read and re-read it, then shook her head.

'So?' he said urgently.

'So?' she replied, in an obvious tone of indifference.

'We must accept!' Joseph said.

'Why must we accept? You know these are not our kind of people Joseph. We don't mix in these...' she waved the envelope in front of his face '...circles.'

'But this is different. Mr Edelson is my boss,' Joseph replied, somewhat defensive now.

'That may be so, but this isn't business. You, we, are not obliged to attend, so if you don't want to, you don't have to.' She dropped the invitation on the kitchen table.

'Oh, but I do want to. And anyhow, it will make a nice change. After all, we rarely go to parties and it would be an insult to Mr Edelson not to.'

'Well, if you insist...' Magda snapped as she resumed her chores.

'Good. Then that's settled,' he said, picking up the invitation and putting it in his coat pocket.

It was a lavish affair. A four-piece band in matching white suits and purple bow ties played popular party standards, as guests milled about in their droves, laughing and joking with the consummate ease of those for whom parties were a perennial pastime. Mr Edelson, who was standing beside Mrs Edelson, a few feet away from Joseph and Magda, was holding court with several employees and their wives, all so garish looking with their big hair and big jewellery. He was much shorter than Magda had imagined – stout, with large hands and fat fingers and a big round face that sunk into his thick neck, so that she couldn't help but stare at him. In contrast, his wife was tall and slender, with long auburn hair and dark, dangerous eyes that flitted about the room, restlessly appraising the competition. She wore a long thin necklace with a large diamond that nestled seductively in her cleavage and diamond earrings that hung like miniature chandeliers and sparkled like stars in the night sky each time they caught the light.

Mrs Edelson smiled, dutifully poised for introduction, as Joseph and Magda approached her.

'Joseph Hamilton. So nice to meet you,' he said, bowing his head, as if in the presence of royalty.

'Nice to meet you too,' she said, her feline smile accomplished and unflinching. Mr Edelson, with his back to her now, began laughing raucously, which seemed to rankle her.

'This is my wife Magda.' Joseph spoke the words proudly.

'How do you do?' Mrs Edelson said, glancing at Magda's neck for the merest whiff of affluence.

'Very well thank you,' Magda replied undaunted and from the look on Mrs Edelson's face, it was clear that she had suffered a minor defeat. She looked around the room with a fluster, then raised her arm and clicked her fingers to summon one of the several waiters weaving in and out of the guests like phantoms. She pointed haughtily to Joseph and Magda.

'Do excuse me,' she said, sniffing the air as she backed away hastily into the crowd.

'Champagne, water?' the waiter said, looking at them in a manner that suggested they were bereft of refinement.

'Champagne!' Joseph replied with a high-spirited spontaneity, as he took two glasses from the tray and handed one to Magda.

'Cheers,' he said tapping his glass against hers.

'Cheers,' she replied with a faint smile.

Just then, Mr Edelson turned to greet them.

'So glad you could come dear man,' he said jovially, placing his hand briefly on Joseph's shoulder. He spoke with an air of authority that self-made men often possess, but there was not a hint of the office surliness Joseph had long grown accustomed to.

'Thank you for inviting us,' Joseph said, suppressing his habitual tendency to pander.

'And who is this vision beside you?' Mr Edelson enquired, his chubby face already flush from too much drink, while beads of perspiration trickled slowly down his temples like tiny pearls.

'This is my wife Magda,' Joseph replied.

'Magda. A lovely name for a lovely lady,' he said as he took a large white handkerchief from his pocket and dabbed his forehead, his eyes all the while focused on something over her shoulder. 'Enjoy yourselves! Mingle!' and without another word, he hastened to the far side of the room.

'How do you like the champagne dear?' Joseph said.

'It's very nice Joseph,' Magda replied and they looked at one another a little lost, as if they had unwittingly wandered into the wrong room.

A few minutes later, one of Joseph's colleagues came lurching towards them, grinning and waving frantically, with the look of someone standing on the deck of an ocean liner about to set sail.

'Well bugger me Hamilton, you came! This has to be a first!' he bawled, slapping Joseph on the back with such force that he toppled forward and spilt the champagne.

'Yes, we came,' Joseph replied genially, curbing his irritation for the sake of his wife.

'Didn't think it was your thing to be honest old man,' he said, smirking.

'It isn't exactly, but...'

'Don't let the boss hear you say that,' he said, nudging Joseph with his elbow. 'And who's this...your fancy woman?'

'This is my wife, Magda.'

'You've got a wife! An ugly old bugger like you! Just kidding. Hello Magda.'

He took her hand, shook it vigorously and winked. 'Oops, empty glass. Time for a refill,' he said and much to their relief, staggered off into the crowd.

As the evening wore on, guests became increasingly animated, champagne still flowing like it was on tap. Mr Edelson and his wife coaxed the less intoxicated onto the dance floor, while the band played a medley of greatest hits that spanned the decades, to satisfy all tastes.

'Let's dance!' Joseph said taking Magda's hand, a little light-headed now.

'No no, I couldn't,' she replied pulling away anxiously.

'Just one,' he said. He linked his arm in hers as he led her through the crowd and onto the dance floor, with a determination she had rarely seen. They danced with sudden abandon, she following his steps as they glided effortlessly around the floor, and it was as though a perfect stranger was serenading her. In no time, her uneasiness at seeing a side to Joseph she had not previously known gave way to the thrill of his hand in hers, while the other was pressed firmly against the small of her back, sending quick shivers down her spine. The guests began to form a circle around them, cheering and applauding as they swept past in their unadulterated rapture and danced until they were giddy.

When the circle was broken and the crowd dispersed, Joseph and Magda sat down to catch their breath.

'One more?' Joseph said jubilantly, raising his empty glass.

'I don't think so,' Magda replied, panting as she put a hand to her chest, a warm glow of contentment rising in her. Her composure not yet restored, she lowered her eyes bashfully as she fixed a few wisps of wayward hair and smiled at Joseph.

'Time to go?' he said, placing his hand on her knee.

'Time to go,' Magda replied.

'It's a lovely evening. Let's walk awhile,' Joseph said and they strolled out into the brisk night air, happy in each other's company. Just the two of them.

MISS MAYHEW'S ARRANGEMENT

The door to Miss Mayhew's apartment on the twenty-third floor faced the lift, so she was long accustomed to the perpetual whoosh of its ageing mechanism, like the dull hum of a steady wind, as it rose and fell in the deep shaft through the day and late into the night.

Many years ago, Miss Mayhew had worked as an editor in a large publishing house in town, until, one morning, she was summoned by the head of department, who informed her, in a most dispassionate manner, that due to declining sales in the paperback division, cutbacks were inevitable and regrettably, she was now surplus to requirements. She was summarily dismissed, with scarcely more than ten minutes to clear her desk and gather the various mementoes that the years had yielded, while colleagues looked on and nodded sympathetically, quietly relieved at having been spared. She had given much of her life to literature, supplanting the sanctity of love for the sanctity of the written word. Books had been her world, but with no job and loneliness looming, she found herself free-falling into a pit of permanent despair.

In the wake of her isolation and the boredom that was its constant ally, it had become her habit each morning to sit on the old green leather chair by the coat stand in the hall, where she drank tea and eavesdropped on the conversations of her neighbours while they waited for the lift. She had reached an age when even the least disturbance gave cause for vexation, but it troubled her not. In fact, her frequent snooping served as a welcome distraction from her now sedentary life and she imagined herself as something akin to a priest in the confessional. Consequently, she found herself privy to not a few intriguing revelations and when, on occasion, her curiosity was sufficiently roused, she would look through the peephole in the door, to put faces to the various voices.

One morning, she heard a conversation between two men, in which one confided to the other how, in a moment of madness, he had gambled away the considerable sum of ten thousand pounds in a casino the previous evening, but had not told his wife for fear of her fury, the marriage already teetering on precarious ground. Lying awake in the dead of night, the magnitude of his predicament almost too much to bear, he relived it over and over in his mind. He spoke of how, drowning his matrimonial woes, he had gone for a few drinks after work before stumbling, somewhat inebriated, into the casino, where, swept away by the heady allure of wealth, he chanced his luck among the high rollers.

His friend suggested he take out a loan and bank the money before his wife discovered it missing. But he felt certain that anyone willing to lend it so readily would insist on such an inflated return, he would find himself in an even worse dilemma. He considered telling her that he had lent the money to a desperate friend who had faithfully promised to repay it in the coming weeks, only to abscond with every penny and not a word from him since. But he knew she would insist on telling the police, who were sure to ask questions, thereby sealing his fate.

For several mornings Miss Mayhew heard the two men by the lift, discussing how to best resolve the problem. She listened attentively, her ear pressed firmly against the door as she hung on their every word. When, at last, she looked through the peephole, she recognised them. The troubled man and his wife lived in an apartment along the hall and she had seen them often. She had come across the second man, a neighbour and confidant of the first, only twice, but had spoken to neither.

When a week had passed with no solution to the problem, Miss Mayhew came upon an idea. She had a substantial sum of money put by for a rainy day, money she had inherited from a cousin of her late mother and which she had never had occasion to use. She could offer to lend him the ten thousand pounds and, with no need of financial gain, thought of how he might pay her back in other, more gratifying ways. She was lonely and now, contemplating life beyond middle age, welcomed a little companionship. The company of a man, any man, would, if only for a while, appease her increasing sense of loneliness.

The very thought of him, a young man, not unattractive, had stirred something in her and so, the next day she waited on the voices of the two men in the hall. When she spied the troubled man through the peephole, she pushed a folded note under the door marked for his attention, in which she told him how she had overheard the several conversations and how she might help. She watched as he bent down to pick up the note. She had seen his name on the brass plate by his doorbell, when it had meant nothing to her. Now, she could think of little else.

As soon as she woke the following morning, she rushed to the door. On the floor were several envelopes, all of them bearing a stamp or postmark, except for one. She scooped them up, hurried to the kitchen and sat at the table. There, written in bold black ink, was a letter from her neighbour, accepting, in the most formal manner, her proposal of companionship, once, possibly twice a week and asking how soon the money could be deposited into his account. Miss Mayhew promptly drew up an agreement, which they both signed and his friend witnessed. He would repay the debt in monthly instalments and when he made the final payment, their arrangement would cease.

And so their unconventional liaison began.

In the months that followed she found him to be a surprisingly affable companion, his furtive comings and goings breathing new life into her otherwise prosaic existence. He was kind, charming and considerate, not a hint of the obligation that could have so tarnished their little arrangement.

She neither saw nor heard the other man for some time until, late one afternoon, she recognised his voice in the hallway. He was speaking in a loud whisper and when she looked through the peephole, was rather surprised to see him in a telling embrace with her companion's wife. Sure that neither he nor his wife were aware of one another's indiscretions, she thought of how inconvenient it would be for all concerned, especially herself, if either of their deceptions were uncovered - the husband mired in debt and bound to contractual amity, his adulterous wife oblivious to his unwitting misdemeanour and his friend, the object of his wife's adultery and party to his unfortunate predicament. All had their secrets and that's how it must remain.

Day after day, Miss Mayhew listens to the careless utterances of misfortune and impropriety as told by the hapless souls behind the door and she waits patiently on new possibilities, new arrangements. She is less lonely these days, for there is always another friend on the horizon, or closer still, on the other side of the door.

FLAMENCO

I

Just after sunset, when a gentle breeze swept in off the Mediterranean Sea, the young boy walked into the town with his mother and father, where every evening a man with skin the colour of burnt leather played guitar outside one of the several cafés in the square. He seldom looked up from under the heavy lids of his soulful black eyes and rarely spoke, save for the occasional *Gracias*, when people expressed their appreciation. The boy watched him studiously, enrapt as he held the guitar close to his body and tuned it with the skill of a virtuoso, while fellow holidaymakers mingled with locals and drank sangria from terracotta jugs, merrily inebriated and all but oblivious to his presence.

He strummed softly at first, his long, sensuous fingers rippling delicately over the strings, as though he was caressing a woman. His playing was barely audible over the bustle of the town square, until suddenly the tempo grew fast and frenzied, his fingers moving so quickly that they seemed to fuse together in a fleshy blur. His knuckles rapped the hollow wood, his foot furiously pounding the floor. A loud, lingering *Ssshhhh* stopped everyone in their tracks as they watched intently, waiting

63

on the fiery finale. It gave the boy goose bumps, his angelic face glowing with unimaginable joy; such intense feelings as his parents had never seen, especially in one so young.

After some time, the man came to know the boy, smiling and nodding whenever he approached.

'He's my friend,' the boy would say to his parents proudly, even though they had never exchanged a word.

One afternoon, as they arrived in the town square, he was sitting outside the café preparing to play as usual. The boy ran over to him.

'Ju like flamenco?' the man said with a gentle smile.

'Oh yes, I love flamenco!' the boy replied excitedly, so happy that his new friend had at last spoken to him.

'What is jour name?' the man asked, in a weary but tender voice.

'Peter. What's yours?' the boy asked enthusiastically.

'I am Miguel. Nice to meeju Peter,' he said, holding his hand out.

'Nice to meet you too Miguel,' the boy replied, beaming as he shook it fearlessly.

'I play this one especially for ju.'

The boy watched attentively, as the long bronzed fingers began to play, each pluck of the strings sweeter than anything he had ever heard, sweeter even than his mother's voice; then the unbridled tempest that followed and rose to a spine-tingling crescendo that quickened the little boy's heart.

When Miguel had played his last tune, the boy turned to his father and held out a cupped hand. His father took a few coins from his pocket and gave them to his son, who threw them gaily into a tattered straw hat on the floor, in front of where Miguel sat.

'See ju tomorrow?' Miguel said, winking at Peter's father.

'See you tomorrow...' Peter said blithely, looking back at Miguel and waving frantically as his mother took his hand and led him away.

On the last day of their holiday, as his parents were busy packing he begged them to take him into town one more time, to say goodbye to his friend.

When they arrived, Miguel was nowhere to be seen and Peter dragged them around, insisting they look in the cafés and up the narrow side streets that ran off the square. They enquired among the locals, who laughed, before telling them that he didn't surface until late afternoon and was probably sleeping off the booze, as usual. But the boy was distraught, refusing to leave until he had seen his friend and when at last Miguel appeared, unshaven and dishevelled, Peter ran up to him and threw his arms around him.

'Miguel Miguel, I found you!' he said.

'Hey, Peter, my friend,' Miguel replied, rubbing his eyes and blinking in the dazzling light of day.

'I'm going home today,' Peter said, bravely fighting back the tears.

'Do not be upset Peter. Ju will come back one day, si?' Miguel said, his voice still hoarse from the previous night's intemperance.

'Oh yes, si,' Peter said.

'Good. I will be waiting for ju my friend.'

'Play one more tune Miguel, just one more...for me,' he asked, his small hands clasped together pleadingly.

'Okay Peter. One more for ju. But first, Miguel needs coffee.'

Peter watched him as he disappeared into the café, his silhouette swaying unsteadily in the darkness. He poured himself a coffee and took a hip flask from his pocket. He unscrewed the top, poured the contents into the cup, then threw his head back and drank it down in one gulp. He fetched his guitar from behind the bar and as he emerged, caught the eye of Peter's father. Realising that he too had been watching him, he smiled apologetically and shrugged.

Miguel sat outside in his usual spot and began tuning the guitar, holding the neck to his ear as he picked on the strings. Sweat glistened on his forehead and trickled down his temples into the deep lines that framed his bloodshot eyes. A small crowd started to gather and as Miguel began to play, the boy's bottom lip trembled with emotion and his eyes filled with tears.

He played erratically, tired and hung over, but the boy didn't notice. He only saw his friend, his hero, making magic one last time.

When he had finished, Peter ran towards him, the tears streaming down his cheeks now.

'I'll never forget you Miguel...never,' he said and they hugged one another in farewell.

'Time to go,' his father said as he clung zealously to Miguel.

'Go with your father now,' Miguel said, ruffling Peter's hair as they parted.

The young boy turned several times, waving at Miguel until he could no longer see him.

II

The quaint little town that Peter remembered from his childhood was different. There were more cafés and souvenir shops, and hotels where olive trees had once flourished, and yet a warm familiarity swept over him, as though time had stood still.

He was married now, with a child of his own, but he had never forgotten Miguel, never forgotten the beautiful, haunting sound of flamenco guitar echoing in the balmy night air, and as he crossed the square, he wondered what had become of his friend.

Immediately he recognised the café where Miguel had played each evening more than thirty years ago. It was one of the few places that had remained unchanged, the paintwork still scorched and peeling from neglect.

Peter walked around the square and asked in the various bars and shops if anyone remembered Miguel, or knew of his whereabouts. He spoke to the elderly gentlemen who spent their days playing cards in the shade of a pine tree, and to pretty young waitresses who stood outside the cafés handing out menus with photographs depicting the various local delights, but no one seemed to know or care and his heart sank at the thought of not seeing him again.

It wasn't until his last evening, as he walked into town

with his son, that he saw a figure in the near distance, approaching the main square from one of the side streets. In the half-light he could tell it was an old man, his hair grey and dishevelled. He moved slowly and with a stoop, his bloated belly, like a sack of sand, weighing him down. Peter took his son's hand and steered him in the direction of the old man, picking up pace as he got closer.

'Miguel! Is that you?' Peter called, rushing towards him now. The old man stopped in his tracks and looked up at him, his eyes squinting in the orange glow of evening. He stood for a moment, stroking his chin as Peter neared. When his eyes widened, Peter's heart quickened, just as it had done all those years ago, and it was then that Miguel saw him.

'Miguel, it's me, Peter!' he cried.

'Peter? My friend?' he said, a look of astonishment on his face.

'Yes, Miguel, your friend.'

'You have returned!' Miguel held out both hands to receive him.

'Yes,' Peter said. The two men embraced for several minutes and it was as if he was that same little boy once more.

'I'm still here,' Miguel said triumphantly. 'How do I look, eh?' He turned this way and that, patting and cradling his fat stomach, like an expectant mother.

'You haven't changed a bit,' Peter said laughing.

'Ha. But ju...ju are a man! And who is this?' he said wincing, clearly in pain as he slowly bent forward to meet the child.

'This is my son, Michael. I named him after you,' Peter said proudly.

'After me? What an honour! Ju look just like your Papa,' Miguel said, pinching the boy's cheek.

'Do you still play Miguel?' Peter said, a wishful, childlike longing in his eyes.

'No. I cannot. Ju see.' Miguel held out his gnarled hands and shook his head, then linked Peter's arm as they strolled across the square to the old café.

'Everything is the same and jet, is changed. Si?'

'Si,' Peter said.

They sat for most of the evening in silence, happy at seeing one another again and when, from time to time, they spoke, Michael listened attentively to stories his father had told him many times before. But there was a persistent sadness in Miguel's eyes, a look that Peter remembered, but as a child had not understood.

It was late when they said their goodbyes and the square was almost empty, but for a few drunken revellers, singing heartily as they made their way back to their lodgings.

'Can we walk you home my friend?' Peter said, placing a hand on Miguel's shoulder.

'I am an old man, but my legs, they are still working,' Miguel replied, a rare twinkle in his ebony eyes, and as he slowly shuffled off down the narrow side street, Peter knew it would be for the last time.

JIMMY

The old blue bus tore along the empty coastal road, depositing billowy clouds of thick black smoke in its wake. When it came on a shallow ridge it juddered and the passengers, already weary from the midday heat, bobbed up and down like limp rag dolls. Country music blared out of an old CD player that was taped to the dusty dashboard, while the driver, a corpulent, scruffy man with greasy black hair that clung to the nape of his neck, whistled loudly out of tune, though no one dared challenge him.

She read magazines and did crossword puzzles to pass the time and tried not to think of home, or Jimmy, who would be missing her now and sure to be blaming himself, convinced he had said or done something to make her leave. The customers would be curious too, asking why she hadn't opened up shop and wondering why the familiar smell of warm bread wasn't wafting into the street at the usual hour. And poor Jimmy would have to explain, except that he couldn't.

Only a few nights earlier they were in the pub, making plans for when the visitors flocked to town for the summer festival, talking about how they'd set up the small forecourt in front of the shop and have music and dancing late into the evening. Jimmy would be lost

71

without her. He had told her many times before. 'You'll be just fine,' she'd say, putting a comforting arm around his shoulder, her words already a harbinger of her intention.

'I never know what you're thinking Suze,' Jimmy would reply in a light-hearted tone usually reserved for the customers, but you could tell by the way he paced back and forth as he spoke, busying himself restlessly, that he meant it.

When they were kids, she and Jimmy spent hours playing in the woods that backed onto his house, especially in the summer, when it seemed to them like a magical forest. But one day it was as if a little of the magic died, when she saw him kissing another girl, and even though she knew the girl had goaded him, had exploited his weakness, down the years she would remind him of the day he broke her heart, an unforgiving look on her face as she said it. It was a look he would never forget. And when she knew she had punished him enough, she would laugh and ruffle his hair, like he was that same helpless boy again. No, Jimmy never knew what she was thinking.

'It's so hot in here,' the young man next to her said, fanning himself with a paperback so tattered it could have passed through many hands.

'Yes...it is,' she replied, looking up from her crossword. He had a pleasant face, with a kind of openness about it, and she could tell he was angling for conversation. She thought about how in different, happier circumstances, she would have liked to talk, would have enjoyed a bit of friendly banter with the ease of someone who had nothing in particular on their mind. Instead, she cast her eyes back to the crossword, frowning as she chewed on the end of her pencil, to give the impression of being occupied.

'Sorry,' he whispered and she smiled.

It was nightfall by the time the bus reached its destination and there were great sighs of relief when the driver flung the door open and the cool evening air blew in. People sat up with a renewed vigour and scrambled to get at their bags, elbows and limbs nudging each other as they fumbled under seats to find their shoes. Then the mad rush for the door. Susie sat awhile, waiting for the gangway to clear, the young man still beside her in the aisle.

'Ev'rybody off!' the driver shouted, cursing the passengers as they stepped down from the bus when they failed to tip him.

'Good luck,' the young man said as he made his way to the door, hastening his exit in order to avoid the spitting invective of the driver. Once outside, he raised a hand to her in farewell and she smiled again as she walked down the aisle and watched him disappear into the night, the wheels of his suitcase rattling on the cobblestone street as he went.

She had booked a room at a small guest house close to the bus station only days before and in the near distance, as she stepped down from the bus, she recognised the illuminated neon sign above the door that read 'Comfy Inn'.

Soft light emanated from the windows of the several rooms and when she entered, a pretty, doll-like girl was standing behind the front desk, affecting a welcoming smile, one side of her face warmly lit by the tangerine glow of an old-fashioned table lamp.

'Help yourself,' she said, directing her eyes to a glass dish filled with boiled sweets.

'Thank you,' Susie replied, taking one to oblige.

The girl led her up a narrow flight of stairs to a modest room on the first floor.

'Anything you need, just dial zero,' the girl said vacantly, then skipped out of the room like a young child. Susie switched on the bedside lamp and set her case down on one of the twin beds that were pushed together, as if a couple had been expected. She climbed onto the other bed, switched off the lamp and was soon asleep.

The next morning on her way down to breakfast her first thought was of Jimmy, poor Jimmy, the last person she would ever want to hurt.

She stood by the door of the small dining room that looked out onto the street and waited until, presently, a middle-aged woman with a pitiful expression led her to a table by the window and handed her the menu.

'Coffee, tea?' she said, her woeful expression unaltered.

'Coffee please,' Susie replied with a broad smile, in an effort to assuage the pervading gloom.

The few other guests talked quietly among themselves, occasionally looking at her, as if she had done something shaming. She gazed out at passers-by on their way to work and thought of how Jimmy would be opening up shop and waiting anxiously for her, just as he always did. She couldn't say what drew her to this place. She might as well have closed her eyes and stuck a pin in a map. Perhaps it was the name, Windflower, but her only thought had been to get away.

After breakfast, she strolled into town and wandered along the high street, looking in shop windows. Everything seemed so cheerless, even the mannequins, in their summer dresses and colourful jewellery, as the early sun quickly disappeared behind a big grey cloud, adding to the dreariness of it all.

Walking back to the hotel, she bumped into the young man who had sat beside her on the bus.

'Hi. Remember me?' he said a little coyly.

'Hello. Yes, of course!' she replied.

'I haven't noticed you around here before.'

'No,' she said.

'I guess you don't live here.'

'No, just visiting.'

'Well, it's not the most exciting place in the world to visit, unless of course...do you have family here?'

'No, no family. And you?' she asked, more out of politeness than interest.

'Me, I'm born and bred here. Lived here all my life. My great granddad came here first, so you could say we go back aways. Of course, it was a lot different in his day.'

'I can imagine,' she said and smiled.

'I don't know how long you're around, but if you

happen to be free this evening, howsabout a drink?' he said with a sudden pluckiness as he doffed an imaginary cap.

The thought of sitting alone in her room, staring at the walls, suddenly filled her with dread and although a big part of her had gone there for solitude, for time to think, another longed for a little adventure, a temporary distraction from all that troubled her. He looked at her intently while she pondered his proposal, his pluckiness slowly waning.

'Sure, that would be nice.'

'Great!' he said, the relief in his voice palpable. 'Now, you see that pub over there...The Finch,' he pointed at an unattractive black building across the street, 'I'll meet you there at seven. There's live music on Friday nights, so maybe we'll even have a bit of a boogie, or whatever you fancy.'

'See you there,' she said.

'Hey, I don't even know your name,' he said, edging towards her as she began to walk away.

'Susie...I'm Susie.'

'And I'm Ryan, pleased to meet you.' He shook her hand firmly, as though they had just closed a deal.

The pub was already packed to the rafters when they arrived and there was a steady murmur of excitement in the air. The band was setting up on a raised platform in the corner, adding to the sense of anticipation. Most of the men were dressed casually in jeans and t-shirts, but their girlfriends were done up to the nines in mini skirts and towering heels, as if they were in a nightclub.

'They're a blues band,' Ryan said, tilting his head

towards the stage. 'But they do a bit of pop as well, to please the younger punters. Wait here. I'll be back in a mo,' he said and disappeared into the crowd.

She thought of how it was just like the pub at home where she and Jimmy went once or twice a week, except that the old Rock-Ola, the landlord's prized jukebox, was the only entertainment.

He returned with two glasses of white wine.

'By the time I got to the front of the queue,' he said handing her one, 'I realised I'd forgotten to ask what you wanted, so I guessed.'

'You guessed right,' Susie replied.

'Cheers!'

'Cheers.'

As the band started tuning up, the voices grew louder, so that everyone was shouting in order to be heard.

'What do you say we sit over there? It's a bit quieter,' Ryan said, pointing to an empty table by the fire escape.

'Sure,' she said and followed him through the crowded bar to a table from where the band were just visible.

'So, what's your story Susie, or would you rather not say?'

'I'm not sure I have a story really,' she answered.

'Oh everyone has a story,' he said.

'Well, I come from a close-knit community, where everyone knows each other,' she said wistfully.

'But that's a good thing, isn't it?'

'Sometimes, sometimes not. It can be very claustrophobic.'

'Only if you let it,' Ryan said, a gentle lilt in his

voice.

'I had to get away for a while, a change of scenery, that sort of thing.' She spoke the words decisively, in a way she hoped would discourage his curiosity.

'Is it a fella?' he asked.

'No....not exactly,' she said and laughed. 'Although there is someone I'm close to. We grew up together, but there's never been anything between us.'

'I see. And is that the way you want it?'

'Yes. No. I don't know.'

'Ah.' He turned and looked in the direction of the stage. 'They're about to start. They usually open with Brown Sugar. That always gets everyone on their feet,' he said and Susie felt relieved at not having to answer questions she wasn't sure she had answers to.

It was almost midnight by the time he walked her back to the hotel.

'Thank you for a great evening,' she said, conscious of the doll-like girl eyeing them from behind the front desk.

'Don't mind her. Hey, howsabout lunch tomorrow? I'll show you round town. It won't take long,' he said with a wry smile.

'Thank you. I'd like that.'

'I'll come by at twelve thirty,' he said and sauntered off blithely, one hand in his pocket, the other waving until he was out of sight. She ignored the unsettling gaze of the girl as she ran up the stairs, tipsy.

Alone in her room, she felt overcome by a mix of sadness and guilt. She would call Jimmy in the morning, tell him not to worry and let him know she was okay.

78

Then she'd ring Josie and ask her to help in the shop, just like she always did when one of them was sick.

The following day Ryan was waiting for her at the front desk, winking at the doll-faced girl as he pocketed a few sweets from the dish.

'Good afternoon Miss Susie. I will be your guide for the day,' he said, looping his arm to be linked as Susie descended the stairs. The doll-faced girl rolled her eyes skywards and tutted.

'Have fun,' she said in a monotone voice all but devoid of sincerity.

By one-thirty the tour was over and they were sitting in the patisserie having lunch. The smell of fresh bread, emanating in waves from the small open kitchen, reminded her of home and of Jimmy. She thought of him in his despair, because she had called to say she wasn't coming back, at least not yet. Then there was the quiver in his voice on hearing hers and the way he had tried to sound so valiant, so as not to add to her burden of guilt. That was Jimmy for you, kindness itself.

'A penny for them,' Ryan said.

'Sorry?'

'Your thoughts, a penny for them,' he asked, even though he could read her mind.

'I was miles away.' She shook her head and gazed into the distance.

'Will you be staying a while?' he said, a conspicuous hopefulness in his words.

'I don't know. I have a lot to think about, except I don't want to think about anything.'

'Look, I know it's not my business and stop me if

you want, but what exactly are you running away from?'

'To be honest, I'm not sure' Susie said. 'All I know is that I had to get away, had to distance myself from everything, from the day to day, the same old same old.'

'Well, I hate to be the one to tell you this, but that's life. Not many of us get to do the things we most aspire to, the things we dreamed of doing when we were kids. Still, we find a way to make it work, to make the most of the hand we've been dealt,' he said cheerfully.

'Wise words for a young man,' Susie replied.

'I study the philosophers,' he said, before conceding that he had in fact read it in a small book of daily affirmations that he picked up in the charity shop in the high street for fifty pence, and she smiled, happy to have made his acquaintance.

She didn't see him again for some time. Instead, she stayed in her room, or took long walks outside the village to clear her head. He dropped a note in at the hotel to say should she fancy a drink, she could find him at The Finch on Fridays and sometimes Sunday lunchtime, especially when roast beef was on the menu. But as the days passed, her only thoughts were of home. Poor Jimmy, she kept telling herself. Poor, faithful Jimmy. Growing up together they had been close, too close, so much so that they had become inseparable and it was assumed they would one day marry. *You two not tied the knot yet?* people would say when they came into the shop, and *isn't it about time?* She and Jimmy laughed it off, but in the back of her mind, she wondered what it would have been like if they'd married and had children, and even though Jimmy never said anything, never once made a pass, she knew, deep down, that he loved her, knew he would jump at the chance of their being an item. She had wanted to see more of life, to have a few boyfriends, to travel and do all the things young girls do, but it never quite happened that way.

She and Jimmy had helped in her mother's shop on Saturdays ever since they were fifteen, and when they left school, they both ended up working there full time. It was all she and Jimmy had known. Then fate played a hand. Her mother died after a brief illness and from then on, she was bound to the shop, just as she was bound to Jimmy.

One afternoon she bumped into Ryan in the village.

'Here she is,' he said heartily, a big grin on his face.

'Hi Ryan. Good to see you.'

'I thought you'd hibernated, but no one hibernates in the summer, do they?'

'No, I don't suppose they do,' she said laughing.

'Fancy a coffee?'

'Sure, why not.'

Several hours later she had told him everything, about Jimmy, her mother, the shop, the words tumbling out of her as though she had just broken a long vow of silence. She had never met anyone with whom she found it so easy to talk, not even Jimmy, and she thought of how hurt he would feel if he knew.

'You're a good listener Ryan,' she said.

'The listening's easy. It's the talking that's hard,' he replied with a knowing smile.

She remembered when she first thought of leaving, the day a customer, a stranger, came into the shop. He hung around for a while, flirted with her and bought things he didn't need in order to linger, then playfully asked her to run away with him. She laughed as he stood outside, blowing kisses and making faces through the window, while Jimmy sulked. Perhaps that innocent encounter had in some way been the catalyst, because it was then that she knew she must go, even though she and Jimmy had been apart just once, when his grandfather was dying and he had gone to him in his final hours.

She had begun to feel homesick, but it wasn't just home that she was missing now. It was Jimmy. She called him every few days, each conversation harder than the last. Worse still, something in his voice told her that he was beginning to resent her for having left, that he could no longer live in a state of limbo, waiting and wondering when, or even if, she would return. In all the years she had known him, he had never expressed himself so utterly, so fearlessly, and it was then that the thought of losing him filled her with dread.

'I think it's time to go home and face the music,' Susie said to Ryan in the pub one day.

'I'll miss you,' he replied in a spirit that told her he had been expecting it.

'It's Jimmy. I couldn't bear the thought of his not...his not caring for me anymore...his not...' she said, her voice faltering.

'Loving you?' Ryan said, drawing the words out of her.

'Yes, his not loving me,' she said looking away

uneasily. 'I just hope he can forgive me.'

'Oh, he'll forgive you. You know he will.'

'I suppose I'd better go if I want to be home by dinner,' she said, staring into an empty glass.

'You're a fine lady, a fine lady for sure. Jimmy's a lucky man.'

'Thank you Ryan. Thank you for everything. We hardly know each other really, but you've been a friend, a good friend, just when I needed one.'

'Glad to have been of assistance!' he said in his usual cheerful manner, clicking his heels and saluting her, even though she could tell he was hiding a sadness of his own. He took her hand and shook it warmly.

'I think we can do better than that,' she said and hugged him. Then she kissed him softly on the cheek.

Back at the hotel, she called Jimmy, to tell him she was coming home.

THE RED HANDBAG

She took the red handbag with her everywhere she went, guarding it with a strange determination, as though her life depended on it. Her neighbours thought her rather eccentric, swapping wildly exaggerated stories about her at dinner parties, while children teased her mercilessly when she passed them on the street.

She was a slight woman with an elfin face and pallid complexion, her mousy brown hair scraped back in a ponytail, adding an austerity to her delicate features. Her clothes were dark and drab and, consequently, one's eye was instinctively drawn to the handbag.

As far as anyone knew, there had been neither a husband nor children, but any curiosity concerning affairs of the heart was all but eclipsed by a much greater interest in the handbag and moreover, its contents. Rumour had it she kept it by her bed while she slept, so that people wondered if it might be harbouring something of a sinister nature, like a gun, or the spoils of a criminal past.

She came and went alone, the handbag firmly anchored to the crook of her arm. On the odd occasion, she smiled at a familiar face, but spoke to no one, and it was as if she lived an otherworldly existence.

There was someone once. He was tall and slim and quite ordinary but for his eyes, which were a luminous, emerald green. His name was Robert, a name I liked. It reminded me of an actor I once admired. He was kind and attentive, in a way that ordinary people often are, and he made me feel beautiful, even though I knew I wasn't.

The first time I saw him was at the house of an old friend, one evening in early spring. I remember the precise moment he walked into the room, because he had to stoop to pass through the low arches of the old cottage, with its heavy oak beams and latch doors.

I was standing alone for some time, studying a rather uninteresting portrait that hung above the fireplace, in an attempt to mask my uneasiness, when he came over and introduced himself. He spoke softly, in a near-whisper, and by the way he looked at me, I knew he liked me. He asked what I thought of the portrait. Not much, I said. He laughed and without the slightest hint of indignation, told me he had painted it.

Soon after, we began seeing each other and it was as if nothing and no one else mattered. We were rarely apart and in no time I could hardly remember my life before him.

One day he arrived on my doorstep with a large box covered in bright floral gift-wrap. He watched intently as I opened it. Inside the box was a red handbag, the most beautiful handbag I had ever laid eyes on. He told me he had seen it in a shop window and pictured us strolling together, me close beside him, one arm linking his and the other proudly clutching the bag. It had a small handle and an old-fashioned pearl clasp, and the cream satin lining had a lovely smell of newness about it. I looked in the several compartments, wondering what I could fill them with. He laughed and told me that a lady with whom he was once acquainted had advised him that if a man wished to learn anything about a woman, of her character and of the things she most cherished, he should look inside her handbag, because the contents of a woman's handbag speaks volumes about the woman herself. Not me, I said coolly, longing to be different. Well then he replied, you must fill it with your imagination, with your dreams, and I laughed. Think of it as a vessel to hold all the things that are dear to your heart and when you feel sad, or lonely, you can simply open it and be transported.

We shared many happy times together, everything we did an adventure, from a walk in the park to a casual dinner. But it wasn't to last.

One day, he disappeared quite suddenly, like a thief in the night, and it was as though he had never existed.

From that first evening, I had sensed the mystery in him, shrouded behind those emerald green eyes.

I never knew how long it would be before the fairy tale ended. Perhaps that's why every moment was like a gift. Looking back, it seemed to me he had come into my life like a celestial being, come to give it purpose.

I waited for him in the hope that he would one day return, but I never saw him again.

I've become very attached to the red handbag, and although it is filled with nothing but dreams and memories of our time together so long ago, it has transported me, just as he promised, and taken me places I might never have been.

THE BLIND DATE

He marched towards me all pomp and swagger, checking his reflection in shop windows and running his fingers carefully through a head of sleek blonde hair as he neared. There was a touch of the dandy about him, a well groomed self-assurance.

'You must be Caroline,' he said, his arms outstretched in the spirit of a long lost cousin.

He wore a cream linen jacket, coral seersucker shirt, blue jeans and caramel loafers. Mr Continental. Except I knew he was from Croydon, because Deborah had briefed me the night before.

'Matthew, pleased to meet you,' he said, thrusting his hand at me like he was directing traffic.

'Pleased to meet you too,' I said taking it. It was warm and clammy and his strong, lingering grip sent a cold shudder down my spine. I was already beginning to wish I hadn't come.

'Sorry I'm late. I'm a stickler for timekeeping, but I was halfway down the road before I realised I'd forgotten my Oyster card,' he said, slapping his forehead with the palm of his hand.

'No problem,' I replied, smiling readily in an effort to mask my mounting regret.

'Now, let me guess...' He took a short step back, pursed his lips and caressed his chin thoughtfully. 'Looking at you, I'd say you're a white wine girl.'

'Actually I'm more of a red wine girl, although I never say no to a glass of bubbly!' I said defiantly.

'Bubbly it is then!' he chirped, with implausible abandon.

We sat at an old wooden table that wobbled when you leant on it, which he did several times to emphasise the problem.

'Two glasses of your very finest...your best...house champagne!' he called to the waiter, in a tone that alluded to arrogance.

'I thought French bistro might be your style. Debs told me you favoured informal and well, it's very casual, very authentic don't you think? They don't even give you a side plate for the bread,' he said boastfully.

The waiter brought the champagne and poured it into two small flutes of such ordinariness they all but muted any sense of occasion, then lit the tea light that was wedged into a shot glass in the centre of the table, which Matthew was now attempting to steady with his foot.

'To us,' he said, tilting his glass to meet mine.

'To us,' I echoed with reluctant sincerity.

'Debs tells me you're keen on the theatre.'

'Yes,' I replied, 'I do enjoy a good...'

'I went to a comedy in the West End last year,' he cut in. 'I think they call it farce, don't they? Anyway, it was lots of people pacing back and forth, shouting at one another and slamming doors. To be honest, I didn't find it very funny.'

He ordered cashew nuts and olives and ate most of them himself, gorging on them like someone who hadn't eaten for days.

'Did Debs tell you she and I almost got it together once?' he said, as he scooped the last of the nuts from the bowl, threw them into his mouth and licked his fingers.

'She might have mentioned something,' I replied vaguely, too alarmed by his glaring lack of refinement to think.

'Between you and me,' he said in a hushed tone, 'I told her, I said Debs, you're a lovely lady and I'd be delighted if you'd give me the honour of taking you to dinner. It was the way she looked at me, a definite hint of mischief in her eyes. So you can imagine my surprise when she thanked me, mumbled something about professional boundaries and said she would rather we stayed friends, because friendships were uncomplicated, unlike love. I only asked her to dinner for Christ's sake, not her hand in marriage! If I can be honest with you Caroline - and I think I can - I couldn't help feeling she was fighting her womanly urges, though I can't imagine why. Mind you, she's at that age,' he said, his squinty green eyes conveying a you-know-what-I-mean expression.

'What age is that?' I replied, eyeing the clock above the bar.

'Discretion dictates I say no more, at least not until we get to know each other better,' he said winking several times, as if something had just flown into his eye.

The waiter hovered expectantly, then removed a pencil from behind his ear. He pointed to a blackboard on the wall and began reciting the specials as though in the depths of utter despair, his downturned mouth adding to the apparent apathy – 'Moules Mariniere - Soupe de poisson - Tartare de thon avec ses legumes de Provence.'

'French,' said Matthew 'is so much more romantic than English, don't you think?'

The waiter rolled his eyes.

'Do you speak French,' I said, certain that he didn't.

'Not exactly,' he said. 'But if I did, it would be at the top of my list, followed by Italian and not forgetting Spanish of course. I'd love to speak Spanish. I know a few words. Buenos dias. Buenas noches.' He laughed. It wasn't funny, but I laughed too. It seemed polite.

'Excusez-moi,' the waiter said, replacing the pencil behind his ear as he backed away.

'Nowadays I tend to holiday in the Caribbean. Well, once a year anyway,' Matthew said proudly.

'That's nice,' I replied and he went on to tell me how, ten years ago, in the good old days, as he called them, he won Salesman of the Year.

'A week in Barbados and I never looked back! Problem is, these young guns are everywhere. Take your eyes off the prize and you're out,' he said. 'It's a cut and thrust world. You've got to get what you can when you can. Survival of the fittest, that's my motto.'

'Quite,' I said.

He opted for the fish soup and I had tuna.

'Avec pommes frites!' he declared with an air of unworldliness.

'Yes,' I replied, straining a half-smile.

'Well, this is nice,' he said, noisily slurping his soup.

'Have you done this sort of thing before?' I asked.

'Oh yes. I've met some lovely ladies, but for some reason we didn't seem to click. I'm not sure why, because I don't normally have any complaints, if you get my drift, Caroline.'

'Really?' I replied.

'Oh yes,' he said raising an eyebrow, the irony of my remark lost on him.

Now and then his foot came off the leg of the table and at one point the soup splashed from his plate and onto the napkin that was tucked into the collar of his shirt.

'Phew, that was close,' he said, mopping his brow with the corner of the napkin.

'Hmm,' I said, as he sucked the last of the soup from his spoon.

'Cost me sixty quid this bloody shirt.'

He suggested dessert, summoned the waiter with a raised hand, then clicked his fingers like Zorba the Greek. The waiter looked at him and sneered.

'They do a good tarte aux pommes,' he said, clearly chuffed with the way the words came out, and it occurred to me then that he had almost certainly exhausted his limited command of French.

'Well then, tarte aux pommes it is,' I said, a renewed enthusiasm stirring in me as the end of the evening drew near.

'The thing is,' he said, 'I'm a sensitive man, so I like to think I'm tuned in to a woman's needs. Too eager to

93

please, that's my problem. They don't thank you for it, although something tells me you're different,' he said, grinning fervently as he exercised his brow for a second time.

A MARRIED WOMAN

She met her husband on a weekend break in the Algarve. She wasn't looking for love, but he pursued her with a tenacity she was unable to resist. He was charming, generous and persuasive, the kind of man it was hard to say no to. Within a year, they were married. Her friends gushed about how lucky she was to have such a wonderful, loving husband, one who seldom raised his voice to her, their rare, intemperate exchanges quickly forgotten. And yet she was restless, plagued by a recurring dream that began soon after their wedding day.

In the dream, she was sitting alone on an empty beach. The sand, like sifted flour, was the whitest she had ever seen, and the sea, gently lapping the shoreline, seemed to go on forever. Suddenly, out of nowhere, a gigantic wave would come hurtling towards her and just as it was about to sweep her up and carry her deep into the belly of the ocean, she would awaken.

She told no one about the dream, fearing that to do so would be to reveal too much of herself.

Each morning, she stood by the drawing room window and watched her husband stroll blithely up the garden path and on down the avenue.

She couldn't remember exactly when it started, when her heart shut down and all the things that had so endeared her to him grated on her now, like the scrape of chalk on slate. At times, she felt the guilt so keenly, wondering how her devoted husband, still of the same good nature and the same unwavering passion as when they had first met, could not have noticed that she no longer loved him, could not have detected every nuance of her closed heart. Perhaps it was her compassion, or the compliant smile, never once betraying her true feelings, that had obscured his judgment.

One Sunday morning she went out as usual to buy the newspaper, but consumed with her plight, took a wrong turn and found herself in front of the coffee shop in the high street, looking at a man who was sitting near the window.

Moments later, she was standing beside him.

'Hi,' she said, with the look of someone completely adrift.

'Hi. Do I know you?' he replied.

'No,' she said.

'I didn't think so. I would have remembered if I'd seen you before. I've only been in town a few weeks, so that probably explains it,' he said, sensing her anxiety.

'Yes,' she replied and she felt as if her feet were nailed to the floor.

'I only popped out for the paper, but I was daydreaming as usual, because I turned left when I should have turned right,' she said shyly.

'Well, I'm very happy you did.' He touched her

lightly on her arm and she pictured her husband waiting impatiently at home, wondering what was keeping her.

'Can I buy you a coffee?' he said, then stood and pulled out an empty chair for her to sit.

She remembered the things she had read in the papers about ordinary people who left for work in the morning, never to return; lonely, frustrated people, deeply dissatisfied with their lot, their uneventful lives turned upside down because of a moment's madness, or more hauntingly, a moment's clarity.

In no time he was regaling her with stories of the places he had been, people he had met, of the women he had known and how his nomadic ways had precluded any chance of lasting love and she felt, with an exquisite surge of pleasure, the illicit thrill of being with a stranger. And yet there was a feeling of familiarity, a sense that she had known him for years, and a confidingness in his voice, as if she was the only woman with whom he had ever shared his thoughts.

He asked her to tell him about the things she longed for most in life, about her hopes and dreams, but she couldn't remember and it was then that she realised they had long since been usurped by her role as the dutiful wife, bound in wedlock to the perfect husband.

It was only when she glanced at the clock tower in the square that she realised they had been talking for hours, although it seemed like much less. She knew that her husband would be trying to call her now and she was relieved when she remembered that, in her distraction, she had left her phone on the kitchen table.

'Will I see you again?' he said, aware of her sudden unease. She wanted to say yes. She said it to herself over and over. Yes.

'I doubt it,' she replied, fixing her gaze on him now.

'I thought not. Such a shame, don't you think? Still, I've enjoyed our time together more than I can say,' he said, his words hinting at the unexpected intimacy they had shared so briefly. She was aware of his eyes scrutinising her left hand, settling on the wide platinum band and it was then that she felt as though he could read her thoughts, as though he could reach out and touch the emptiness within.

'I'll be here if you change your mind,' he said, 'but 'I'm only in town for a few more weeks.'

'I'll remember that,' she said, with a casualness that implied their meeting had meant little, even though she knew it had not and he looked at her and smiled ruefully.

For a long time she thought of nothing and no one but him, thankful for the precious time alone when her husband left for work in the mornings and when she could relive the all too brief hours they had spent together, every word he had uttered etched in her mind, filling the lonely void. She thought of what she longed to say to him, of how she wished she had remembered all those buried hopes and dreams and she wondered where his resolutely free spirit had taken him, this man whose name she didn't even know. She imagined him in another city, another country, sharing his stories with other women; women just like her.

She never dreamt of the sea again, or of the huge wave about to engulf her and sweep her off to some faraway place. She dreamt only of the stranger now, the memory of him, his face, his eyes, his touch, unceasing, while her perfect husband slept beside his lonely wife, oblivious to her growing desolation.

LETTERS TO VERONICA

Maya followed the tall portly woman along the narrow stone path that led to Cypress Cottage, bumping into her as she came to an abrupt halt and studied various coloured fobs that were attached to a large bunch of keys. She tried several, then inspected the lock, huffing and puffing impatiently, until at last she found the right one.

'Thank goodness,' she said, brimming with frustration as she prised it off, inspected her nails and mumbled something heatedly under her breath.

Once inside, she hastened down the narrow hallway that led to the kitchen and as they entered, pointed to an old Aga that she insisted, in a somewhat imperious tone, added a particular charm to the place, as did the small Welsh dresser in the corner, which reminded Maya of her grandmother. Beyond the kitchen window was a pretty garden, strewn with a bronzed carpet of leaves that swirled lazily and shimmered in the autumn sun, and she pictured herself sitting on the little bench beneath the crab apple tree on warm summer evenings, listening to the wistful strains of Joni Mitchell.

The woman led her up the stairs and showed her around with great urgency, drawing her attention to the various historical features.

'So, what do you think?'

Maya giggled and clapped her hands.

'It's perfect. I'll take it,' she said.

'Good. I'll draw up the paperwork when I get back to the office,' the woman said, not a hint of congratulation in her voice.

About a month later, after Maya had settled in, she remembered having seen an old shoe box in the cupboard under the stairs on the day she arrived. She hadn't opened it, thinking someone might come by to claim it, but nobody did and now her prying mind had got the better of her.

Several minutes later, she was sitting on the floor, staring at a stack of envelopes, bound together with grey ribbon. She untied the ribbon and laid the envelopes out. Each was clearly addressed by the same hand, in the same blue ink, bearing the same London postmark. But what immediately struck her was that none appeared to have been opened. She gazed at them intently, as if by sheer will she could fathom their contents. Then she retied the ribbon, put them back in the box and replaced it under the stairs.

She thought about the letters often, but dared not read them, until, one evening, no longer able to contain her curiosity, she took the box from the cupboard and opened one.

Darling Veronica, despite our having met only briefly, I cannot stop thinking about you and how beautiful you looked in that crimson silk dress. I fear I may have overwhelmed you with my deep admiration, but I am already so enamoured with you and long to see you! Please have dinner with me. In case you have mislaid my number it's 01735 664212. I eagerly await your call. John xxx

Maya read and reread the letter, all the while imagining Veronica, dazzling in her crimson dress, every man in the room vying for her attention.

That night she didn't sleep, guilt-ridden at having opened the letter, at having been privy to something so intensely personal, and yet she hankered for more. A few days later, she opened another. It was formal and less flattering than the first.

Dear Veronica, I was somewhat surprised not to have heard from you. Yes, surprised, not least because not only did you so readily welcome my company, indeed you encouraged it. You had many admirers eager for your attention, but as I remember, and I remember well, you chose to spend your time with me. So as you can imagine, I am rather perplexed at your lack of response. My feelings are unchanged and I would dearly love to see you. John

And so the obsession began. Every few days Maya opened another letter. Some were affectionate, others disappointed tirades on rejection and unrequited love.

It has been several weeks, he wrote, *since our fateful meeting and I am most disenchanted at your silence. I have, respectfully, never come calling, even though my longing to see you is great. I think of nothing else now and feel I am losing my mind. John*

A couple of months had passed by the time Maya opened his final letter.

Dear Veronica, It is not my way to pursue <u>any</u> woman (he had underlined the word any) *with such fortitude, nor would I have pursued you had I not felt that something extraordinary happened between us that night. And so it now leaves me to wish you well and hope you find what you're looking for. Your greatest admirer, John xx*

Maya knew, the moment she finished reading, that she must contact him and tell him that all his letters had gone unopened.

The next day she rang him.

'John Mallinson,' the voice answered curtly.

'Um…Hi. You don't know me. My name is Maya.'

'Who?'

'Maya.'

'I think you have the wrong number.'

'This is John isn't it?'

'Yes, this is John. Look, who…'

'I don't quite know how to tell you this. It's about Veronica.'

A brief silence followed.

'Veronica? What about her? Do you know her?' he said, the tone of his voice a distinct measure of his surprise.

'Not exactly, no, but I live at Cypress Cottage and...'

'What is this about? Has something happened?'

'Well, when I moved in last year I found a box of unopened letters under the stairs.'

'Unopened?'

'Yes...and all of them were addressed to Veronica,' Maya said, her heart quickening with every word. 'The thing is, I have a confession. I opened them. I'm so sorry. I didn't know how to contact her and I...'

'You read them?'

'Yes.'

'All of them?'

'Yes. Please don't be angry. It's just that, well, once I'd read them I knew I had to call you to tell you that she hadn't. Maybe she left shortly after you met. Anyhow, as I said, the letters were here when I moved in.'

'So, I imagine you have certain ideas about me now, but you have to believe me when I say this: I am not the kind of man who obsesses over a woman, but she was unlike any woman I have ever met.'

'Would you like me to send them to you...or would you prefer to collect them?'

'I wouldn't want to put you to any trouble, but one could say the letters have, albeit unwittingly, brought us together.'

A few nights later there was a knock at the door.

'Hi. You must be John,' Maya said and smiled.

He stepped back, hesitant, his face illuminated by the unsteady glow of the porch light.

'And you're Maya of course,' he replied.

She had not expected a young man exactly, but he appeared much older than she had imagined when she read the letters.

'Have you come far?' she said as she led him down the hall and into the kitchen.

'Not too far,' he replied and she could already sense his uneasiness, because the letters had been so telling.

'Please, sit down,' she said.

He sat at the kitchen table, his large brown eyes slowly registering the room.

'I pictured her here, in this house, many times,' he said dolefully.

'I can imagine. But you never called on her?' Maya asked.

'No. No,' he said. 'I couldn't.'

'But all those letters...surely it would have been simpler to find out if she was still here.'

'If I'm honest, a big part of me knew that she was long gone, but by then I couldn't stop writing. It was like an addiction and all I had to hold onto was the memory of that one night, one single night that drove me on, like an obsession. I know now that in some way I was feeding the fantasy of her, of the possibility of our being together.'

'I think I understand,' Maya said, because reading his letters had consumed her too, though she could not tell him.

'I have to say, I'm rather surprised you asked me here. You don't know me from Adam,' he said.

'Oh but I think I do, in a way. The letters revealed...'

'I wish they hadn't,' he said cutting in.

'I'll get them,' she said, disappearing into the hall.

He wrung his hands together anxiously and looked around again, his eyes focused on a pink teapot on the windowsill and the fresh flowers in a sky blue vase.

Maya had made it home and for all he knew, Veronica may have passed through only fleetingly, as in a dream.

She returned with the box of letters.

'Here. They're all here,' she said handing it to him.

'I expect you think me very foolish,' he said.

'No, I don't,' she replied.

'A man of my age behaving like a star-crossed lover over a woman I barely knew. But you see, I couldn't help myself. From the moment I saw her...'

'We can't choose who we fall in love with,' Maya said a little mournfully.

'That we can't.' He looked away as if to suggest he had said enough.

'Are you going to read them?'

'Not now,' he said.

'I'm surprised they were never passed on to her. Perhaps she lost touch with whoever was keeping them,' she said.

'Perhaps,' he replied.

'How did you know she lived here?' Maya asked with a sudden practicality.

'Well, on the night of the party we shared a taxi home and I dropped her off.'

'I see.'

'She invited me in, asked me if I wanted to stay, but I declined. Every part of me wanted to say yes, but she'd had a few drinks and I didn't want her to regret it in the morning. I didn't want to jeopardise what might have been. I kissed her briefly on the doorstep and asked if I could see her again. She gave me a lingering, almost wounded, look, took an old receipt from her coat pocket and instead of giving me her number, she asked for mine. In my pitiful naiveté, I felt certain we would meet again. So when, several days later, I'd heard nothing, I wrote to her here, at this address. It was, as you know, the first of many letters. Ah well, as they say, there's no fool like an old fool.'

'Maybe fate will bring you together again one day. Stranger things have happened.'

'Oh no. It's much too late for that.'

He placed his hand carefully on the box, as if it was filled with precious jewels. Then he stood slowly.

'I suppose I should be going,' he said.

'I'm sorry, I've kept you,' Maya replied.

'Rather I've kept you.'

'Not at all. I've enjoyed our meeting.'

'Me too,' he said and it was then, by the way he looked at her, that she sensed a shyness in him, a vulnerability that drew her to him.

'I'm about to have a glass of wine. Can I offer you one?' she said and with little hesitation, he accepted.

'I'm making dinner shortly and it would be no trouble to cook for two.'

The thing about being lonely, about loneliness, Maya thought, is that one has an uncanny knack of recognising it in others.

She took a bottle of wine from the fridge and placed it on the table. He watched as she fumbled with the corkscrew, distracted by his sad eyes and gentle smile.

'May I?' he said and she handed him the bottle.

She thought of Veronica, of what might have been had she and John met again. He poured two glasses of wine and gave one to her.

They clinked and drank a toast to serendipity.

THE LOOK OF THE DEVIL

As he stepped onto the train his eyes darted manically up and down the length of the carriage, before settling on the empty seats opposite a fresh-faced girl with curly hair. On one of them he flung a large black rucksack, then sat, belligerently, on the other. Within moments he was stabbing the air with his finger at an elderly lady who was sitting nearby.

'Stoopid old dame. Held up the line in the ticket office. Drove everyone nuts. I almost missed the goddamn thing. This is the airport train isn't it?' he said, glaring at the fresh-faced girl. His manner was brusque and edgy, every syllable delivered like a sharpened dagger.

'Yes,' she replied, 'But it's not the fast one.'

'Jee-zus Christ!' he said throwing his hands up.

She took a book from her bag and pretended to read, but she could feel his eyes piercing into her, sizing her up as he primed himself for confrontation.

'Where you from?' he said, tapping his fingers agitatedly on the table between them.

She peered out tentatively from behind the book.

'Um...London,' she replied, but not wishing to encourage conversation and in order to avoid his disquieting presence, she continued reading.

'I been here two weeks. Two weeks too long. Place is a dump. Thing is, I had to get away, see. I had it up to here,' he said, raising a hand to his forehead as if to shield his eyes from the sun. With his other hand, he lowered her book, so that their eyes met.

'Why London?' she said.

''Cause it's as good a hellhole as any,' he snapped.

There was a thugishness about him, the close-set eyes and snarling mouth, and his forehead glistening with sweat, all suggestive of a fugitive in a spaghetti western. And yet there was something mysteriously beguiling about him, of the kind women fall prey to.

'Used-ta have family here. My mother's sister. Married an Irishman. A drunk. A loser. Had two kids. Little brats. Always gettin' in trouble, but who could blame 'em.'

'So it wasn't them you came to find?' she asked and he looked at her like she had said something damning.

'Hell no! My mother's sister never liked me from the moment the cord was cut. Said I had the look of the devil.' He made a V sign with his fingers, drew them up to his eyes, lowered his head and glared at her.

'Why would she say something like that?' she replied, with a coolness that veiled her increasing uneasiness.

'Maybe 'cause my mother had that same look in her too.'

He backed away from the table, as though he had said enough. She could have left it there, could have seized the moment to retreat back into her book, but now, in

112

spite of her unease, she was curious to know more.

'Where are you from?' she said.

He scowled.

'You always ask so many questions?' he said, each word spoken with the cageyness of someone with something to hide.

'Sorry.'

'New Jersey, born an' bred. Me and Springsteen. 'Except he got rich and I never. Lucky bastard.'

The old lady jolted in her seat, opened her eyes, looked up at him and frowned.

'You got a problem grandma?' he said and she quickly directed her gaze out of the window.

'What don't you like about London?' the girl said. He took his time before answering. There was a faraway look in his eyes, a restlessness.

'It's okay I guess...no worse'n Jersey. It ain't the place, it's the people, right?'

'I suppose so, yes,' she said.

She looked across at the old lady, who was already dozing, her mouth half open, her eyes half closed. She wore a plum coloured beret that was tilted to one side and anchored to her head with a small diamanté clip.

'Stoopid old dame. Look, it's like this...'

Like what?' the girl replied.

'Shut up and I'll tell ya. Jeez.' He began cracking his knuckles one by one, first the left hand, then the right.

'I got a kid at home...Cody...he's a good kid too, a real good kid. It's his mother that's the problem. Always nagging. Always poking her nose where it's not wanted. Just like my mother's sister. What is it with you women?

113

Every one o' ya born with the nagging gene.'

'Not all of us,' she said.

'All o' ya' he replied.

'What did she think about your coming to England?' she asked hesitantly.

'None of her business. We divorced a couple years ago.'

'Oh, sorry.'

'Don't be...I'm not. Woman made my life hell. Bitch. Well, let me tell ya, she's finally got what's coming to her.' His blue eyes flashed with a menacing steeliness.

'What do you mean?'

'Here she goes again with the questions.' He fixed his stare on her, his eyes bulging, deranged-looking and she felt a shudder, followed by a terrifying rush of excitement. He placed his hands flat on the table and leant in closer.

'You alright lady?'

'Yes, I'm fine. I just feel a bit queasy,' she said placing a hand on her chest.

'Wasn't nothin' I said was it?' he asked, smirking.

She felt a sudden urge to escape, to make her excuses, to extricate herself from this strange and dangerous intoxication, but she was helplessly drawn to him.

'You familiar with that Willie Nelson song?'

'Who?' she said, her pulse quickening.

'Jeez...don't tell me you haven't heard of Willie Nelson. You British are all idiots!' he said angrily.

'What song do you mean?' she replied, desperately gleaning all the composure she could muster.

'Funny How Time Slips Away. Best damn song I ever heard,' he said, thumping the table.

'I don't think I know it.'

'What the hell!' he shouted as he leaned back into his seat. 'She's got it comin' to her.'

'Can't you sort things out for the sake of your son?' she said, in a futile effort to appease him.

'It's way too late for all that crap. She coulda stayed outta my life, but she just kept comin' at me. Nag nag fuckin' nag. Found herself another guy, just to torment me. Thought I'd come crawling back on my knees. No fuckin' way.' He waved his forefinger back and forth. 'Poor jerk, didn't know what he let himself in for. A country hick. Regular schmuck. Got a job in one of those lousy chemical plants. Must've messed with his head. Well I've had plenty of time to think since I been here and I got a plan.'

'You're not going to do anything awful are you?' she said frantically.

'Awful?!' he bellowed and at once all eyes were on him. 'What the fuck y'all lookin' at? There's something you don't understand lady.' He leant in again, as if about to impart a shocking revelation. 'She had her chances and she blew 'em, all of 'em. Like I say, I'm up to here,' he said in a low, ominous tone, shielding his eyes for a second time. 'This is just between us kiddo. You and me.'

She prayed for the airport stop.

When at last the train arrived, he yawned like a roaring lion and stretched his legs out under the table, the tips of his boots hitting her shins as he did so. Then he stood, grabbed the rucksack and threw it over his shoulder.

'Well, this is me,' he said, holding out his hand. His grip was tight and she winced in pain until he let go.

As she watched him walk away, she trembled with relief. He stopped by the old lady, moved in close and tugged at her beret, laughing as he did so. She looked at the girl disapprovingly, as though she had in some way been complicit in his malevolence.

He turned to look at the girl as the doors opened, his eyes burning into her, and it was then that he did something that chilled her to the core. He raised his hand to mimic a gun, pressed it to his temple, pulled on the imaginary trigger and laughing, blew on the muzzle of the barrel.

As he stepped off the train, he turned to look at her one last time.

She sees his face everywhere, the piercing eyes, the murderousness behind them a constant reminder. Endless thoughts of him, of the mother of his child, haunt her, harrowing and unceasing, from the innocent chime of the alarm clock, to the moment her head hits the pillow.

Then she dreams of him in her sleep, in the dead of night.

THE WEDDING RECEPTION

It was only supposed to be a small affair but somehow things escalated, thanks to family intervention. And so it was that bride and groom were taken hostage in the unexceptional function room of a hackneyed hotel on the outskirts of London, surrounded by two hundred or so people, most of whom they had never met. If only they hadn't let slip news of their intention and instead eloped to some remote destination, free of the obligatory nuptial nightmare. How they abhorred tradition.

Having survived the somewhat protracted ceremony, with its avowed words of unwavering devotion, they couldn't decide what they dreaded most; the customary speeches with their predictably toe-curling revelations - none of which were vaguely amusing - or the first dance, with all eyes upon them as they shuffled self-consciously around the polished parquet floor, accompanied by a sentimental ballad, with its promise of everlasting love, while starry-eyed females looked on and sighed dreamily with envy.

The best man, an acquaintance of the groom, stood to speak and already in a state of advanced inebriation, he recalled the early days, the bachelor days, as he regaled guests with long-winded yarns of past conquests and debauched exploits; the little one with the big tits, the

117

leggy one with the big arse and the easy one with the big everything, inappropriate stories mercifully punctuated by the popping of corks and the fizz of cheap champagne.

More humiliating tales followed, of boyish pranks and mooning out of car windows after a night on the lash, all of which the groom claimed to have no recollection. The bride smiled sweetly and rolled her eyes, while children scurried about noisily, skidding across the floor in their shiny new shoes and hiding under tables, oblivious to the yawning tedium of the day.

Soon after, a freckled-faced man with red hair jumped up from his chair and, clearly worse for wear, declared his undying love for the woman who had left him several years earlier and who was now sitting across the room with her new husband and squealing infant. The guests laughed uneasily as the man plopped back into his seat, mumbled tearfully and guzzled more wine.

When the party was in full swing, the groom's father tapped a knife repeatedly against his glass and called for silence. The disgruntled band stopped playing and having procured the attention of his fellow guests, he told them he would like to make a special toast to the bride and groom, even though it was a little late in the day for another uninspired salutation. He informed them that he wished to contribute by singing a song, a long time favourite by the late, great Frank Sinatra, one that bore no relevance to the occasion. Then, as would a consummate professional, he nodded to the band leader, who gritted his teeth and clicked his fingers as he counted the musicians in. The groom's father belted the song out, half singing, half croaking at the top of his voice, the veins on his neck and temples raised, ready to pop. Then he threw his arms in the air as he held the last note for what seemed like an age, his complexion a deep burgundy now. Everyone whistled, clapped and stomped their approval as he collapsed into his chair, jubilant and overflowing with pride.

The band resumed playing, the bride's sister kicked off her shoes and in a state of near frenzy, dragged several reluctant guests onto the floor to form a line for the conga, much to the chagrin of the singer, who was crooning his way through a soaring rendition of Love Me Tender.

The bride and groom looked on wearily, desperate for an end to proceedings. But as the evening progressed, guests took it upon themselves to avail the newlyweds of more than a few words of marital wisdom. The most intoxicated proffered salacious bedroom tips, while women of a certain age cited their culinary nous as the secret to a long and happy marriage. They listened with feigned interest and smiled politely, consumed only with thoughts of their departure.

Sometime later, a weary-looking, po-faced woman, whose towering bouffant had spectacularly collapsed into something resembling a compressed bird's nest, came over to acquaint them with the important matter of wedding etiquette. She wobbled unsteadily on pencil-thin heels, her shocking-pink talons digging into her hips, and with an air of self-appointed authority, informed them that in case it had escaped their minds, the bride and groom customarily took their leave before the guests. She stared at them with a blank expression, tapped the face of her watch repeatedly and demanded to know if they planned on leaving any time soon.

How they saluted tradition now!

THE WOMAN IN THE PRIMROSE DRESS

The merciless glare of the afternoon sun could not diminish the enduring beauty of the woman in the primrose dress.

On fair days she could be seen at one of the many cafés that lined the Boulevard Saint Germain, a short stroll from her apartment on the Rue Bonaparte, where she watched the daily procession of passers-by.

In her younger, more carefree days she had enjoyed everything Parisian society could offer, had dined in the best restaurants, drank the finest champagne and indulged in every delight her youthful beauty could muster. But those days were gone and she had long since ceased caring for the things that so beguiled her then.

One warm spring afternoon she was aware of a smartly dressed man observing her from a nearby table. She had been careful not to catch his gaze until, at last, their eyes met and she acknowledged his ready smile with a nod. He was not young, but there was a vitality about him, a presence it was hard to ignore. Suddenly unnerved, she searched her purse for a few coins and placed them beside her coffee cup, but as she stood to leave, he approached her.

'Madame!' he called dashing towards her, bumping

into tables and chairs in his urgency. His voice was rasping, as if every syllable had been wrenched out of him. 'Madame, you can't leave now!'

'I'm afraid I must,' she replied, amused by his fervour.

'Oh, but this cannot be!' He was imploring her now, his arms outstretched, an obstruction to her escape. She shrugged and smiled apologetically.

'Then I shall have no choice but to make you my captive!' he declared. 'We will sit a while longer and drink coffee and talk. Then…' he hesitated, his voice softer now, 'Then we will take a Cognac together and watch the sun go down, no?'

'No.' She smiled, licked her finger and pointed it skywards. 'It's getting cooler and by sunset there will be a chill in the air.'

'Then there's nothing for it but to continue our little discourse inside.' He extended his hand in a sweeping motion as an enticement.

As they entered the café she felt unsettled by the look on the waiter's face (even though she had known him for many years) as he raised his eyebrow in a comical gesture.

'Let's celebrate,' her companion said, clapping his hands and rubbing them vigorously together as though he had chanced upon sudden wealth.

'Monsieur, Cognac! Rest assured Madame that it is not usually my habit to partake of an afternoon aperitif with a stranger, but on this occasion…' He paused momentarily as the waiter set down the glasses and poured the drinks.

'You see Madame, in truth you are not, as such, a stranger, though I fear you may not remember me.' He fell silent as she leant towards him and slowly studied his face, registering each feature as if it were a convolution of tributaries. Then she promptly withdrew and shook her head, perplexed.

'I'm sorry, but I'm afraid I don't…'

'Ah, but of course, you wouldn't!' he exclaimed. 'After all, it was so long ago.'

'But you see, Monsieur, I rarely forget a face, especially one with such character. I don't know how I could have…'

'Well,' he said, with a kind smile, 'time can play such cruel tricks on the memory. A younger, less modest man may even have been a little offended, but I am fortunate. The years have been good to me. In dramatic fashion, he placed a hand on his chest as though about to swear allegiance to some great warrior. 'Alas, even though my poor ego is suffering a small defeat, the libido is still intact. Forgive me Madame. Perhaps I speak out of turn.'

'On the contrary, you are beginning to fascinate me. Tell me Monsieur, what is your name?'

'I answer to Henri,' he said with a flourish of majesty. 'Henri Dumacq.'

She smiled, relieved that his words did not evoke in them some terrible anguished memory, for now she recognised neither the face nor the name.

'And I Monsieur…I am Dominique.'

'Dominique,' he said crossing himself. 'My dear mother's name God rest her soul.'

Having no suitable response, her eyes fell upon the countless photographs of past patrons vying for position on the sallow walls. She had known them well, each with their own story, each bearing witness to the days and nights of shameless hedonism; a prelude to the empty years that followed.

'Madame, excuse my candour, but regrettably we are neither of us in the first flush of youth. You, nevertheless, are extremely well preserved,' he said, his manner akin to that of a seasoned raconteur, 'and may I say, Madame, that it is not that you don't belie your years, but more a matter of my having known you, so to speak.'

'Please, Monsieur Dumacq…'

'Call me Henri…I insist.'

'Well then, Henri…you must put me out of my misery.'

'Dear Dominique...I may call you Dominique?' His full mouth exaggerated every syllable. She nodded her consent.

'One afternoon, many years ago, on this very spot, I found myself captivated by a young girl, a girl so fragile I thought she might snap from a single embrace. She had the look of a Bohemian beauty, her long brown hair copious and wild. She was the most exquisite thing I had ever laid eyes on. She came again the next day and every day after that. I watched her, longing to speak to her, to make my feelings known, to declare this agonising love. For it was agony Madame! But I was young, shy and naive, uneducated in affairs of the heart you understand. Oh, but I do hope these lovesick ramblings are not tiresome.'

'No, Henri, please continue,' she said, an avid curiosity growing in her now.

'Well, time passed and one day I finally summoned the courage to approach her and I told her, with a matter-of-factness that often communicates something of grave consequence, that I had fallen deeply in love with her and that I knew with unwavering certainty that this feeling would never cease. She laughed, thanked me for the compliment and as I walked away, feeling foolish and dejected, she called after me. Even now, I can still hear her words, spoken with such solemnity for one so young - 'Come back in forty years when this so-called beauty has faded and speak to me then about the language of love.'

The woman in the primrose dress raised her glass and smiled at the handsome man.

68067823R00074

Made in the USA
Charleston, SC
06 March 2017